A MAGICAL CHRISTMAS ON THE ISLE OF SKYE

Jodie Homer

Copyright © 2022 Jodie Homer

This novel is a work of fiction. Any names, characters, businesses, places and events are a product of the author's imagination or to be used fictitiously. Any resemblance to actual persons, living or dead, or actual events is purely coincidental.

Cover by Richard Homer

All rights reserved

CONTENTS

Title Page
Copyright
Acknowledgement
Summary
Chapter 1	1
Chapter 2	4
Chapter 3	15
Chapter 4	21
Chapter 5	26
Chapter 6	31
Chapter 7	43
Chapter 8	48
Chapter 9	51
Chapter 10	58
Chapter 11	64
Chapter 12	69
Chapter 13	74
Chapter 14	81
Chapter 15	88

Chapter 16	95
Chapter 17	104
Chapter 18	110
Chapter 19	115
Chapter 20	124
Chapter 21	127
Chapter 22	135
Chapter 23	145
Chapter 24	150
Chapter 25	156
Chapter 26	164
Chapter 27	172
Chapter 28	178
Chapter 29	184
Chapter 30	190
Chapter 31	202
Chapter 32	215
Chapter 33	223
Chapter 34	230
Chapter 35	233
Chapter 36	238
Chapter 37	244
Chapter 38	249
Chapter 39	267

Thank you	275
Trademark Acknowledgement	277
About the Author	281
Social Media	283
Books By This Author	285

ACKNOWLEDGEMENT

I feel like this is an award show, and this is my acceptance speech. Without these people, I wouldn't have a book to be published, so here goes; I would like to thank my husband for his patience and creative skills when I needed help designing my cover.

Thank you again to the Facebook group; Chick Lit and Prosecco, the beautiful and kind people who have helped and supported me.

Thank you Jaimie for all of your funny and inspiring messages you send.

Thank you, Margaret, for your patience and absolutely ace advice. I am totally useless and without you, I wouldn't have a readable book.

Lastly, thank you to everyone who takes the time to read my book and leave me a review or tell me what you think on social media. I really appreciate your support and I hope you enjoy it.

SUMMARY

It takes a village to fall in love.

Set in Scotland, on the Isle of Skye, we meet Harry and Emilia, who have always been best friends, well, until they complicated everything by sleeping together.

Drunk and alone on New Year's Eve, Emilia phones up the TV's psychic and spills out all of her sorrows.

When her friends propose to stay in a cabin in the middle of nowhere for Christmas, Emilia jumps at the chance, but the atmosphere quickly dampens when Harry announces his girlfriend will be joining them. What will happen to Harry and Emilia's relationship when they discover the island is full of old myths and a time loop they just can't escape from?

CHAPTER 1

The man on the TV is annoying.

"Our countdown begins in thirty minutes," he says, interrupting the news segment.

It's New Year's Eve-. Well, actually, it's half-past eleven on New Year's Eve and here I am, alone again. I was invited to my parents' pity party, but I didn't want to be the only one without a date. My friends are all out clubbing, but I have to admit, I'm at the higher end of my twenties and just can't be arsed with clubbing any more.

I put down my bottle of rosé and jumbo box of mince pies, a bargain that was knocked down from £3 to 50p and listen to the two people on the TV.

"We'll now say hello to our New Year psychic!" says Grant Holdman, the balding news anchor, who is sitting a little too snugly next to his guest star.

"Hello and Happy New Year." Mystic Alice looks like she has just stepped out of the 1500s. She's wearing an old-fashioned style dress, with braided hair tied in ribbons.

"Lonely hearts of England, I want to hear from

you. Have you recently broken up with someone?" I think her hypnotic voice has a slight Scottish accent to it. Unless I'm drunker than I thought.

"Whatever reason you're alone, give us a call," she says enthusiastically.

No. I can't. I shake my head, feeling ridiculous. What can this woman do for me? I stare at the phone. Although maybe it would give me answers?

Woof.

"No, Rog," I say, and giggle and stroke the head of my little border collie Rog. He's having none of it and nudges the phone. Giving in, I dial the number and nervously wait.

Roger gives me the side-eye from his little chair, obviously proud of himself.

The phone rings on the TV making me jump, and I realise just how drunk I am. Maybe this wasn't a good idea after all.

"Well, well, Mystic Alice, it seems you have a caller." Grant claps his hands, looking amused.

"Hello there." The voice echoes through the phone and TV simultaneously. I turn the TV volume down.

"Hi," I say.

"What's your name, my love?" she asks.

Before I can say anything sarcastic and tell her she can stick her stupid "powers" where the sun doesn't shine, I slur, "Emilia."

"And, Emilia, what can we help you with today?" Grant says, smirking. He's clearly enjoying my misery. I look at Rog, who now has his back to me.

The shame.

"Well, I've been sleeping with my best friend," I say, and the TV image of Mystic Alice silently nods for me to continue. "And I feel so confused. I don't know if I like him,"

Alice's eyebrows furrow as she listens.

"Well, Alice, what do you make of that?" Grant asks. He is mocking me. I'm too drunk to care, although I know I will regret it in the morning.

"Emilia, you need to think about how you really feel about this person," she says and looks at me through the TV. It's like she can see inside my soul and a shiver goes up my spine.

"Do you want to be with him, or do you want to let him go? I want to know, do you have a history with this person?"

"Yes. No. I don't know… I'm so confused," I say. Regret slowly creeps over me like I'm being submerged in water.

"To save you going round and round in circles, tell them exactly what you've told me. You might be surprised," she says.

"Yes, well, that was an interesting phone call." Grant interrupts her and the phone line goes dead. They've already forgotten about me and are moving on to the next caller. I cringe as I think of what I've just told the entire country. What if my family and friends heard it? I think I need more wine.

CHAPTER 2

I wake up with a head like thunder. New Year's Day. YAY! I survived my first New Year on my own. Rog is whining by the door, so I get up - and a flashback of last night hits me. Fleeting memories of the phone call to the TV psychic which I struggle to piece together. I remember downing another bottle of wine and falling asleep on the sofa. *Oh god.* I cringe at the phone on the table next to the chair I slept on. Did that really happen? How humiliating!

I feed Rog and take two paracetamol. Today is Mum's special New Year's Day get-together. Like a two-day party - but today is mostly about the food. Of course, bastard – Harry - will be there. Harry is my childhood best friend who happens to live next door to me but things are strange between us. We're still kind of best friends, but like I told the medium on the TV: when we sleep together, it messes with my head. *I'll stop sleeping with the bastard – Harry*, I tell myself. I must. And maybe look for someone new.

Dressed in comfortable jeans and a jumper that definitely isn't a Christmas jumper (because who wears one of those on New Year's Day?), I head to my little car with Rog in tow and a small overnight bag. I'll probably get way too drunk to numb the pain of Harry being at the party, and everything will get really awkward. Then I'll end up sleeping over, but I'll be damned if I end up in bed with - Harry. I will not. I slam my hands on my steering wheel.

The drive to Mum and Dad's isn't far and I arrive before any of the non-family guests. Of course, my big brother and sister, Dan and Lucy, are here already. They've slept over from yesterday; well, actually, they arrived on Christmas Eve and haven't left.

Poor Mum and Dad.

"Emilia honey." Mum never shortens my name.

"Hi, Mum, and Dad," I say.

Dad comes in from the garden and throws his arms around me; and we have this awkward three-way hug.

"You should have come yesterday," Dad says. "We saved you some turkey."

Rog wags his tail and his ears prick up. He doesn't know many words, but chicken and turkey are etched into his brain and he starts going mental as Dad puts down a plate for him.

"You look painfully skinny." Mum says and purses her lips together.

"I hope you haven't been drinking too much." She leads me outside into the chilly January air.

"Of course not, Mum," I say, rolling my eyes

behind her back. Dad disappears to get dinner. We always have New Year's salad every year with Billy Bear ham, even though we are all over or nearly thirty.

"So, why are we out here freezing our nuts off?" I ask.

"Language," Mum barks. "Because it's a nice day."

"Crappy New Year's, love, have a drink." Dad hands me a glass of Buck's Fizz and clinks his glass against mine.

"Hi, Lucy." I say with a smile. She's wrapped in a coat and scarf.

"You're the baby: tell them to have dinner inside before my toes fall off," she says and I laugh. We're both the dramatic ones.

"You big wusses," Dan replies, messing my hair up.

"It's fu- fucking freezing," I say and sit down. The plastic is practically frozen.

"Swearing." Mum shakes her head. "Honestly, do you lot have any other vocabulary?"

"No, Mother, their vocabulary is limited by their low intelligence.' Ow!" Dan shouts and Mum shoots us a glare.

"So Emilia, any romance news?" Mum asks. Dad starts bringing out bowls and pots full of New Year's Day salad and Mum gets up to help him.

"No," I say, hoping someone else joins in the conversation.

"Well, love, you don't want to end up like that nut job that was on TV last night." Dad says and shakes his head, serving up turkey trimmings. My head bobs up and my cheeks redden.

"Oh yes, I heard her." Lucy is giving me a suspicious look.

"Who?" I ask, pretending I know nothing.

"Some drunken nut job, wasn't she?" Dan says with a smirk on his face, and I cringe, sinking deeper into my seat.

"Well, I think she must be really sad and lonely," Mum says

Lucy looks at me and I turn away. It's like the cogs are turning in her head and her face lights up.

"Nah, Mum, a complete loser." Lucy looks me up and down.

"Lucy Westbrooks, don't be so mean." Mum slops potatoes onto Lucy's plate. I stick my tongue out at her like the mature adult I am.

"I'm just saying they must be a loser to spill out their entire life on the TV." Lucy sticks her tongue back at me.

Dan is looking between us and hasn't cottoned on yet.

"What?" he says.

Lucy gestures and whispers.

"No fucking way." He whoops.

"Daniel." Mum looks seriously unimpressed, and Dad's eyes flit between us.

"It was you," Dan says, and he and Lucy high-five.

"It was her," she says.

"What was her?" Mum asks.

"The sad loser on the TV last night," Lucy says.

Mum looks at me, her eyes boring into me. It's one of those times you want the ground to swallow you up.

"Emilia, is this true?" Mum asks, and I feel prickly, dirty, like I'm sharing a big secret. This is all too much. I sip some more Buck's Fizz, hoping someone else will hijack the conversation.

"Yes," I mumble.

"Oh, for crying out loud. I thought you were busy for New Year?" Her face is full of concern.

"Hello?" says a voice from next door. Two more plates are placed on the table with glasses of wine. One is on my other side.

"Hello, Cathy." Mum greets our next-door neighbour, Harry's Mum; Harry stands behind her, shuffling his feet, his hands in his pockets.

"So, are you sleeping with him?" Lucy whispers.

"Shut up," I hiss, and she laughs.

"This is too good," she says.

Bastard - Harry is standing with his arms crossed and I'm pretty sure he didn't watch me on TV last night, making an absolute twat of myself.

"Hi," I say with a smile.

"Hello." He sits next to me and I offer him a glass of Buck's Fizz. The surrounding air is strange and I'm on edge. What if Lucy or Dan say something?

"Happy New Year," I say to him, and we tuck into the food.

I'm thankful the conversation around the table

has changed. Mum and Dad are talking about going back to work tomorrow and, if I'm honest, I'm absolutely dreading it.

❖ ❖ ❖

After dinner, I make my way through the house, nudging my annoying siblings out of the way of the radiator. Harry is following me around like a lost fly.

"Rog, my dog," Harry shouts when he sees Rog, and Rog jumps all over him. What a traitor! Harry fusses Rog's belly, while Rog lies on his back.

Mum has set the living room table up with snacks and drinks.

"Emilia, darling, you aren't wearing jeans to the party, are you?" Mum asks.

"No, Mum." I say and roll my eyes and down my remaining Buck's Fizz. Harry catches my eyes as I'm about to head upstairs. I smack my empty glass on the sideboard.

"Do you need some help?" he asks at the bottom of the stairs, inches away from my face. I look into his eyes and my heart races like it always does when we get this close. My head fills with the idea of us being together again.

"No, I fucking don't. Piss off," I shake away the thought. I will not sleep with bloody Harry- the - Christmas jumper-and-tie-wearing-arsewipe.

Rog follows me upstairs into my childhood bedroom with Groovy Chick stickers on the wall.

Mum has reorganised my suitcase and has taken out my little red dress with the leg slit. I'm not dressing to impress. Would she kill me if I came down in my PJs?

"Are you sure you don't need a hand?" A voice behind the door asks. *Fuck's sake.* Rog barks by the door until he sees Harry and then turns into a squirmy mess as Harry rubs his belly again. I look at them both, feeling deflated, and let out a puff of air. Rog is such a whore to him.

"No." I turn around and shimmy into my dress. I swear his eyes light up like it's Christmas. See, this is the problem with sleeping with your friend, isn't it? Most people would be like *good for you, but no, it has its downsides,* like the way Harry is staring at me right now.

I turn to face him. He moves closer. This is dangerous territory. We've tried this before and it was too strange. We couldn't transition from friends to boyfriend and girlfriend.

Harry opens his mouth like he's about to say something, but then changes his mind. Even Rog is fed up with us now and is curled up on my bed, snoring.

Bloody men! Who needs them?

I spray myself with a little perfume and go back downstairs to see our friends have arrived, all dressed up. It was only supposed to be a small party, but Mum always invites my best friends: the crazy people I've known my whole life.

"Em." Razor comes over and does some weird fist

bump thing with Harry and me.

"Em." Tammy, my best friend – and Razor's girlfriend -comes in next.

"Happy New Year, Mrs Westbrooks," says Annie, who's an almost famous artist now, with her own gallery.

"Hello, everyone," Mum says.

Annie takes off her coat and goes straight for the drinks. She is my kind of girl.

"Someone has just been d - u - m - p - e - d," Tammy says.

"I can spell, you know, and it was mutual." Annie comes back over. Her glossy black hair is in plaits.

"Sure it was. You just caught dickhead Dave with his pants down and nothing happened," Tammy says. Annie downs her glass.

"Why don't you go on a date with Harry?" I slur. Shit, how many glasses of Bucks Fizz did I have?

The silence is a killer. No one wants to date someone who wears a tie with a Christmas jumper.

"No, our Annie likes dickheads," Razor says helpfully.

"There's a compliment in there somewhere," I say to Harry, who just shrugs.

"I am so over, men. If Zac Efron appeared right now, I would tell him to jog on," Annie says.

I roll my eyes.

"Em wouldn't, would you?" Tammy asks, and I shake my head.

"I would ditch you losers in an instant," I reply. Mum has changed the CD to what sounds like a kids' school disco soundtrack.

"Come on, guys." Mum herds us into the living room where Lucy and Dan are embarrassingly doing the 'Macarena' by Los Del Rio.

"We used to be ace at this." Tammy joins in.

"Not for me." Harry puts his hands up, leaving us to it.

It's funny, watching a 6-foot man with a green Mohawk and piercings all over him do the Macarena, but Razor has been practising and I can't help but giggle.

"I don't dance, I drink," says Annie.

I join in next to Tammy and Razor. Who the fuck cares? No one will remember this in the morning.

The song changes to The Cheeky Girls and that is too much for Razor.

"Come on, slut, you don't get out of this." Tammy drags Annie and me onto the dance floor to do The Cheeky Girls dance. I daren't even look at Mum's face right now, but I can see her out of the corner of my eye giving Tammy *the look*.

I'm not drunk enough for this one. Even Harry is watching with an amused look on his face.

"Mum, where did you get this CD from?" I ask, as bloody 'Agadoo' by Black Lace comes on and Dad dances with Dan.

"The Pound Shop, love. Everyone seems to like it." Mum is having a great time. She loves hosting parties and everyone is laughing and talking.

Mum puts 'One for Sorrow' on by Steps and starts dancing wildly with Dad.

"Raze?" Tammy asks, and he reluctantly stands up and downs his bottle of Bud Weiser.

"Fancy a dance, Annie?" I ask, trying to lighten her mood. She's been grumpy all evening.

"Sure, why not?" She grabs my hand and we twirl each other around like we are five-year-old princesses again.

"You'll be okay, Annie," I say, as we all dance awkwardly together.

"Why can't I like normal men, Em?" she asks. That's what we've been asking her for years.

"Fuck knows," I say.

"Can I have this dance?" Dan comes over and takes Annie's hand. Annie's face lights up and as they walk to the dance floor, Annie gives me a thumbs up.

Razor has now crashed on the sofa, leaving me and Tammy without dates, and Harry is awkwardly shuffling along the floor.

"You know I'll rip his throat out if he hurts our Annie?" Tammy says, scowling at them dancing. It could be the drunken state we are in, but I think they look good together.

"I know," I say. I don't want to be in the middle of that relationship.

"Anyway, what about you? Are you seeing anyone?" Tammy asks

"No."

"Well, Harry has been watching you most of the night," she whispers,

"Tam, we're friends."

She puts her hand up.

"At least dance with him. He looks so pathetic it makes me want to cry." She pushes me in his direction.

"Hey." Harry says with a smile, taking my hands. I roll my eyes.

I nestle against Harry. *Not good.* He holds my waist as we sway around the room. Tammy eyes us the entire time, and I'm desperately trying to avoid eye contact with her. Mum is dancing with Dad and Lucy is watching me suspiciously.

Harry leans down and whispers into my ear.

"Bedroom."

I nod, ignoring Tammy's curious look. Surely one more night with him wouldn't do any harm?

CHAPTER 3

Eleven months later.

It's the first of November and, for once, we all have lunchtime off together. We're finally going to meet Claire, Harry's new girlfriend. I don't think I've ever been so nervous in my life: I feel sick and shaky.

I leave Rog happily sniffing around Mum and Dad's sweetshop and wave goodbye to Mum and Dad. Outside, the freezing icy drizzle has blown leaves into the air. I don't want to work for my parents forever. I just can't decide what I want to do - and it's a job, after all.

I walk up the ramp and straight through Tesco to the other end of the shopping centre. The aroma of chicken and spices hits me. I've arrived at Nando's and my stomach knots.

I quickly find everyone and we all hug and say hello. Everyone is here in their work clothes.

"Are we ready to order?" Annie asks. How does she stay so slim when she eats like a competitive eater?

"We should wait for Harry," Razor says, looking dapper in his grey suit and tie and styling it out with his green Mohawk. He works in law with his dad, who deals with the firm in Scotland whilst Razor deals with the affairs here.

"Here he is," Tammy says and in walks Harry. He looks around and when he finds us he smiles. His eyes rest on me for the longest and I feel dizzy.

"Thank god," Annie mumbles and looks at the menu.

"Hello everyone," Harry says, greeting us all.

Claire smiles awkwardly at us. She has long blonde hair that looks like it's been dyed. She's slim and pretty in the pinkest clothes I think I've ever seen.

"Hello." Tammy is the first to speak. "I'm Tammy." She embraces Claire, who freezes, then hugs Harry. Razor steps up next and Annie holds her hand up to say hi.

Claire sits next to Annie and Harry, and I sit opposite them, next to Tammy and Razor. We're in a little side booth with cushiony green chairs. I look at Harry, who seems deep in conversation with Claire, as we all look at what food we want. Claire doesn't want spice, but Annie does. Does Claire know we're exes times about ten? We're more on and off than Ross and Rachel.

"So, Claire, what do you do?" Razor asks when we finally order and are waiting for our drinks.

"I am training to be a beautician," she says. Harry squeezes her hand. We all make the appropriate oohs and aahs.

"Her dad is my boss at the bank," he says, and we

all nod.

"I've been looking forward to meeting you all." She says.

"The feeling's mutual," Tammy replies.

"Of course," I say.

I should say something; otherwise, she'll think I'm rude.

"You must be Emilia. I've heard so much about you," she says, and we shake hands. Harry's face is glowing like he is pleased we are getting along.

Before I can make sure it's decent things he's been saying about me, our food arrives: a massive tower of chicken we all immediately pull apart. Claire has ordered a small vegetarian burger.

"Claire, do you want any of this?" Razor asks after we have taken all the chicken and Annie is smothering hers in BBQ sauce.

"I'm a vegetarian," she says quietly, and we all start laughing that we came here.

"Sorry." Annie shrugs and stuffs her face with BBQ chicken.

"Why didn't you arrange to meet us somewhere else?" Tammy asks, her blue eyes twinkling.

"Because we all like chicken," Harry says. The atmosphere is slightly awkward.

"It's okay. I won't preach to you all for eating meat," Claire says.

"Good, because we definitely aren't vegetarians." I bite into a piece of chicken. Harry and Claire are annoying me; of course she's a fucking vegetarian.

"No, we aren't," Harry says while he eats his

chicken. I feel tingly and excited. Something I haven't felt since New Year.

We slept together on New Year's Day after getting drunk and then promised we would try again. We tried for weeks; I thought we were good, and then Harry met Claire. I was devastated. It's almost broken our friendship. For the first month Tammy, Annie and Razor had to see us separately, then slowly we began talking again - but now we're at that awkward stage, where I don't know where I stand with him.

"So, Razor, you wanted to talk to us?" Harry asks after we've finished our food and Claire has popped to the ladies.

"Yes. My parents are letting us use the log cabin for Christmas." Razor looks at us excitedly around the table.

"Really?" Annie asks, licking the sauce off of her fingers.

"In Scotland?" I ask, surprised, then dread prickles me. A whole Christmas with Harry. I know the others will be there, but I'll still be with him. In a cabin.

"No, in fucking France. Yes, of course Scotland," Razor replies, rolling his eyes.

"It sounds amazing, babe," Tammy says.

"It does," Annie agrees.

"Can I ask Claire if she wants to come?" Harry asks, and I feel prickly. This is going to be fun. Though, it isn't like I have to go. I could say no, but then I'll miss out on spending time with my friends. But do I want to spend Christmas with Harry and Claire?

Claire comes back from the bathroom and we all look at her.

"What?" she says looking around at us all and blushes.

"Do you want to spend Christmas with all of us in Scotland?" Harry asks.

"Really?" She looks around at us.

"Sure," Razor says.

"The more the merrier," Tammy adds.

"Well, I can't think of a better way to spend Christmas, and I need some inspiration for my art," Annie says.

"Is that your job?" Claire asks.

"Yes," she says. "Did Harry not tell you I have a gallery?"

"No. He said you painted. That's amazing," she says.

Even with the conversation flowing Claire looks uncomfortable. How serious can they be if we're just meeting her?

"Annie is the shit," I say to Annie.

"I am the shit," Annie announces proudly.

"So, do you want to come?" Harry asks.

"I don't want to intrude," Claire says, blushing.

"You aren't intruding," Razor says.

"It'll be nice to get to know you," Tammy says, standing up. "I have to get back to the surgery." She hugs all of us, including Claire, who seems a bit surprised.

"I should probably get going too," Claire says, and she smiles at us all before sharing a kiss with Harry. Annie makes sick noises and I giggle.

"She seems... nice," I say, trying to think of something nice to say.

I finish my drink. Annie smiles reassuringly at me. I think she understands I am struggling a little with all of this.

"I knew you would like her, Em." Harry beams and I can't think of anything to say. He looks at me, and his smile reaches his eyes. I have to hold my breath to take my mind off of being with him.

"Of course I do," I say eventually, with as much enthusiasm as I can manage.

"If all else fails, at least you'll have a free holiday," Razor says.

"Yes, of course, thank you Razor," I say, and Annie nods.

"You'll love it." Razor pats my shoulder and gives it a gentle squeeze.

CHAPTER 4

It's the night before we leave. I've shut up the sweetshop with Mum and Dad, who aren't happy about me leaving for the whole of December, but have reluctantly given me the time off until I said Harry would be there and then they practically shooed me out of the door.

"Oh, honey. You'll have the best Christmas of your life," Mum says. Her eyes are shiny.

My bags are waiting on the side of the road, and Rog is sniffing around the bushes. I feel sick. I'll be spending Christmas with Harry, but not just Harry: Harry in love. I think back to last month when we were eating in Nando's and in walked Claire. Annie calls her Elle Woods from *Legally Blonde.* After they left, I spent the whole time asking Annie what was wrong with me and what did I do wrong?

Not my best day.

I can't help thinking Claire really won't have a clue about Scotland. Does she realise how cold it gets? I think about Harry. Is he really in love? Did he ever want to be with me?

A feeling of dread builds up in the pit of

my stomach as I think how much time we will be spending together - but as awkward acquaintances, not actually together.

I stare at the few houses decorated on the street in Christmas lights and wish I could turn back the time to New Year's Day again.

Razor parks up at the side of the road with Tammy and Annie. Mum makes him wind down his window. I look inside. *Oh, no.* There's no room for me.

"Now, make sure you look after her," Mum barks at Razor, who salutes her.

"Of course, Mrs Westbrooks."

"And no drinking." Mum aims that one at me. Tammy winks at me. She's packed the entirety of her alcohol cabinet.

"Of course not," I say innocently.

Harry pulls up in the car behind Razor. Rog goes crazy, jumping up the side of the car. When Harry gets out to greet my parents, Rog tries to lick him.

"Harry, darling." Mum greets him with one of her enveloping hugs and red blotches appear on his cheeks.

"So, are we following you, Raz?" Harry asks. Razor puts his thumbs up.

I look inside his car. *No Claire.*

"She's joining us in a few days," Harry says, reading my mind.

"Right." I get in and help Rog into the back.

"I have snacks, crisps and McDonald's in the

car," he says. Rog seems to understand and cocks his head. I almost say I love him, but that's inappropriate.

"Cheers, big ears," I say instead, and he grins.

I sit down next to him and cringe. What do we even talk about?

I am feeling nervous and I don't know if it's because we are driving through the mountains in the dark.

Harry starts the car. What if we have to go through the mud? His car isn't made for that.

"You realise where we are going, right?" I ask, doing up my coat.

"Of course." Harry flicks the heating on.

"If we get stuck in the mud, I'm going to murder you."

It's already cold and soon we'll be in the countryside with no lights. And I'll be alone with Harry. *Fuck's sake.*

Rog is asleep in the back of the car, snoring softly. The silence is nail-biting. I don't know what to say to him.

"Em, are you okay?" Harry asks finally.

Isn't that the fucking question of the century?

"Yes." I wish we could just teleport there, and then I could just simply ignore Harry for the rest of the holiday. Why can't we turn back to that bloody night? I sigh involuntarily.

"We are going to be spending a shit ton of time together, so if there's anything, just talk to me," he says softly; it's almost a whisper, and I daren't look at him.

I hate this atmosphere we've created. We've gone from flirty fun to serious, and now I don't know how to get back again.

"Do you want a drink?" He looks over at me. Thank God he's ditched the Christmas jumpers.

"Yes."

He hands me a bottle with a note from Tammy. I take my phone out to thank her. When we arrive side by side in a traffic jam, she puts her thumbs up.

"Am I that bad you need to be drunk to be in my company?" Harry asks as he watches me swig from the bottle.

"Of course not. I just don't enjoy being in the car at night," I say, and it's the truth.

❖ ❖ ❖

When we arrive in Nottingham, we stop in a random free car park to eat our McDonald's. I let Rog out for a wee. It is fucking freezing outside. I'm wearing a coat and two scarves.

"So, Em, do you want to take charge of the radio?" Harry asks when we put our rubbish away.

"Sure," I click through the channels. It's weird how the city is slowing down now we are reaching eight pm. We still have a long journey to go. Harry wraps another scarf around himself and smiles, making me feel things. I'm not going through this again.

"Here we go." Slade starts playing through the car, lifting our spirits, and we sing along. I have drunk a little more than I thought I had. The alcohol is relaxing me and I have finally warmed up.

"Ready to hit another city?" he asks.

"Let's play truth or dare," I suggest.

CHAPTER 5

It's midnight. We've been on the road for hours and have finally arrived in Edinburgh. I'm feeling cranky from being in the car for too long.

"So, truth?" Harry asks. We are getting dangerously close to personal, but it feels like we are getting closer than we have in ages.

"Yes." I say and bite my lip.

"Okay, if you had to kiss Boris Johnson or Simon Cowell, who would you pick?"

"Oh God, Simon, no question."

Harry's mouth wobbles as he smiles. This is the friend I love. Maybe love isn't the right word.

"Ok, what do you want? Truth, dare, double dare, kiss, command or promise?" I ask.

Harry's quiet for a second whilst he thinks about it. We drive past more trees and the countryside in the darkness.

"Kiss," he answers finally. I look out of the window and giggle.

"I dare you to kiss the cow in the field." I point to the darkness. "On the lips." He chuckles slowing down the car.

"You know, no one has asked me to kiss a cow before." He gets out of the car.

"Happy smooching," I say and giggle. I watch him fade into the darkness. Razor's car stops and he rolls down the window.

"Everything okay?" he asks. Annie and Tammy are asleep.

"Yes, Harry is going to kiss a cow," I say, hearing him swear. When he comes into view, he's wiping his face.

He's covered in what looked like slobber and I can't stop laughing.

"Ew, mate, why?" Razor asks.

"She asked me to." He joins me.

Razor just raises his eyebrow and winds his window up.

"You are a bitch for doing that." He takes a cloth out of the glove box.

"You smell absolutely rank." I hold my nose, trying not to heave.

"Go figure." He backs out of the farm car park and carries on driving behind Razor's car.

"Okay, truth, dare, double dare, kiss, command or promise?" he asks.

"Truth." I'm more than a little tipsy and would not choose it if I was a little more sober.

"Okay truthfully. What do you think of Claire?" The air between us becomes stale and I look out of the window at the darkness with only a little light casting from the moon above.

"Why do you care what I think?" I ask finally.

He looks at me. His brow furrows and his features set.

"You're my best friend. Of course. I care what you think," he says.

I'm silent. I barely know the girl. I've only seen her a few times.

"Em?" he asks. I'm too drunk and too tired for this conversation right now, or maybe I'm not drunk enough.

"She's nice." I say, choosing my words carefully.

I hate the silence. It feels strange. Like we have gone backwards in repairing our friendship and I don't like not knowing what Harry is thinking about.

"Harry," I say, and then take a breath because I see how he's looking at me. Is this how I want him to look at me?

"Em," he whispers.

Harry stops the car and shuffles closer to me. Confused and drunk, I lean in closer to him and the butterflies return to my stomach. Harry kisses my cheek, but I turn and he catches the corner of my lip awkwardly.

How fucking embarrassing.

We drive awkwardly for what feels like forever with just the radio on with the news droning on. I don't know what to say to him. Should we talk about this?

"Why don't you try some music?" Harry finally says and we flip through the stations. Mariah blasts out, and the mood lightens up.

◆ ◆ ◆

We finally arrive in front of the Isle of Skye Bridge, which stretches for miles. Below is the small village of Portree with little rows of cottages in front of the sea that stretches out for miles. The temperature has dropped even more. It's almost pitch black apart from little street lamps dotted around the village and the moon casting light into the sea.

"Wow." I say, looking out of the window. Rog starts whining and pawing at the window, so I wind it down for him to lean out of. The air smells fresh and bitterly cold.

Harry switched the radio off half an hour ago to play a James Blunt CD that he's currently singing along to whilst we weave in and out of the little country roads towards our cabin.

◆ ◆ ◆

We eventually turn into a huge driveway that's bigger than my entire flat, with trees lining both sides, and park behind Razor in front of the cabin.

Harry turns the music and the heater off, and we step out of our cars. Rog sniffs at the unfamiliar smells. His tongue wags to the side.

"Can I sleep here instead?" Annie says with a yawn and pulls her hat and gloves on.

The air is chilly with the wind whipping around us. The clouds look like they're threatening rain and the only light is from the porch.

"Come on, you big baby." Razor rolls his eyes. Every time he returns home to Scotland, his accent comes back.

CHAPTER 6

I wake up next to Harry. The regret from last night is sitting heavily with me.

When we arrived, we were too tired to sort out sleeping arrangements, and I quickly realised there weren't enough beds. Not only that, but Harry insisted I take the bed - and then he must have slowly crept in at some point in the night.

Rog is curled up between us in a little ball, fast asleep.

Through the small gap in the curtain, the sky is still midnight blue, and the moon is still bright. Does it ever get light here?

I sit up. I can feel Harry's leg hair tickling me. Harry stirs when I lift the quilt.

"Are you fucking kidding?" I ask.

"What?" He sits up and rubs his eyes.

"You're naked." I say and gesture to his body, my head scrambling all over again.

"Well yeah. I got too warm," he says. His face is frowning like he doesn't understand why I'm upset.

"What if they come in?" I ask.

Harry sits up. "Jesus, Em, it isn't like anything

happened." He stares at me and I gulp tears. Is this how my fucking Christmas is going to be?

"No because you have a fucking girlfriend," I say.

"Is this what this is all about?"

Huge ugly tears start splattering the quilt and I turn away to focus my gaze out of the window. Of course it's what this is about.

I don't speak, and he wraps his arms around me.

"Em, I'm sorry."

Is he sorry for how he dumped me?

I turn to face him and feel my stomach sink again. Of course, he wasn't going to kiss me. I feel like a prize idiot.

"I'm sorry." He lifts my chin to look at him.

I sigh. I need to sleep on my own tonight.

"Morning, losers." Annie flings open the door dressed in a fluffy green dressing gown and *Elf* pyjamas. Rog snaps his head up at the sudden noise but lays back down when he sees it is Annie.

"Hi, Annie." I say and smile, happy for the distraction. I daren't look at Harry again. Instead, I follow her across the creaky hallway and into the open-plan living area with its huge windows displaying the driveway. The view is like a Christmas card with the mountains and countryside.

"Hello. Is anybody home?" a very Scottish voice shouts from behind the door. Razor's mum and dad, Connie and Fergus, appear in our living room. Tammy and Razor are already sitting in front of the TV with the news on quietly.

I sit next to Harry who has come to see what's happening.

"What time do you call this son?" Fergus asks.

"Oh dear, Ranulph. Why aren't you dressed?" Connie says and tuts at his dressing gown. Razor's mum is very strict, but they've always treated us like their children.

"We've only just woken up, Mum," Razor says while yawning.

"Well, you'd better get a crack on, hadn't you? Breakfast won't wait forever." They both wave to us all before they leave.

"Oh, babe, you know they mean well." Tammy pulls him into a kiss that makes the rest of us look away. It makes me think of our embarrassing kiss. I am so disappointed and embarrassed.

"I'm bloody starving," Annie says and walks into the well-stocked kitchen. Razor said we would have everything we needed, and he wasn't kidding.

Razor's Mum and Dad had brought us breakfast because we were irresponsible adults that couldn't make breakfast for ourselves.

"Do you want to see if the cabin has a Christmas tree in the attic?"

"Sure," he says with a smile at me and I feel my heart thumping.

The others are in the kitchen, helping themselves to the array of food on the table. Cereal in little boxes, along with plates of steaming bacon and eggs. The kitchen smells amazing and my stomach rumbles.

"So, what are we doing today?" Annie asks, shovelling food into her gob like she's never eaten before.

"I'm going to look around the village," Tammy says.

"We need some Christmas decorations," Razor says.

Razor hands us a leaflet that his Mum must have brought in with her. There's a table top sale at the church.

"Are you coming with us, Annie?" Harry asks, but she shakes her head.

"I have to figure out something to paint while I am here," she says with a sigh.

You'd think with all the scenery and greenery around us, Annie would snap them up to paint, but I'm sure she'll spend the day hijacking the living area with her paintings and, when Annie is in work mode, nothing comes before that.

"Don't worry, An, I'll get you some booze," Razor says.

They high five and I sit down, nibbling some of the food that Connie brought around.

I follow Harry to the car after breakfast. Rog starts jumping up at the window. "We should bring him with us. Let him sniff around," Harry says, opening the car door. Rog springs into the car, marking the back seat before curling into a ball.

"Of course," I say and then giggle and sit down

next to Harry.

◆ ◆ ◆

The journey into the village takes less than fifteen minutes and the whole way, we sing along to the Christmas radio station. The surrounding air is cold and I feel very festive today.

The church is situated in the middle of the village, with a stretch of grass overlooking the port. Little cottages are dotted around the winding roads with the owners outside putting up Christmas decorations.

"Ready, Em?" Harry asks and our hands brush as we get ready to leave the car. My stomach flips and my heart races. I try to ignore it as I put a lead on Rog and we get out of the car. Rog immediately uses the grass as a toilet and we walk up the little hill to the church car park that's already quite full.

Connie and Fergus are in the entrance doorway, handing out drinks in little plastic white cups as we walk inside. No one has said we can't bring in Rog, so he trots next to us obediently on his lead.

The church is full of various little stalls, with delicious food and drink smells wafting around. Rog is in his element. In the corner of the church is a small jewellery stall selling beautiful, hand-crafted dream catchers.

"I don't think there will be Christmas decorations." I look around.

"Never mind," Harry says and we brush hands again. This time, he folds his hand around mine. I'm still not happy with him.

"Harry," I say. Why do I feel the way I do?

"Let's get the shopping out of the way."

We walk to a stall with jewellery hanging on little hooks. A woman dressed smartly with a clip in her hair walks over to us.

"Hello, I am Glenda, the local councillor and all round event manager of Portree. I hope you enjoy yourself today. Get your man to treat you." She winks, then looks between us; we're still holding hands.

"Oh, we aren't…" I start.

"No, we aren't," Harry confirms. He pulls his hand away and shakes Glenda's. "I'm Harry."

"Emilia," I say.

"It's nice to meet you both." Glenda says and then walks away leaving me uncomfortable.

It makes perfect sense. If anyone else saw us holding hands, they would think the same. But why did he just snatch his hand away? Is he embarrassed of me?

I hover around the jewellery stall, looking for presents for the girls. I find a beautiful, unique-looking ring and a silver bracelet and pick them up.

"I'll get us something stronger," Harry says, nodding towards the coffee cups. Oh god, why am I feeling so awkward?

I pay for the jewellery and wait for Harry.

"A little tipple for you," he says and we clink our

plastic cups together. I'm not entirely sure if this is wine or not, but I'm grateful.

I look around; spotting a stall that makes me uneasy. I grip Harry's hand tightly.

"Are you okay?" he asks, his brow furrows.

"Yes," I choke out, and Rog pulls the lead over to the stall with the crystals and dream catchers.

"Hello. How can I help you?" says a voice I recognise and Rog barks at her. She flashes us a friendly smile but fixes her blue eyes on me. A shiver travels down my back. Mystic Alice. The psychic from the TV.

"I'm just looking." I pick up a couple of beautiful sparkly crystals.

"So, do you collect crystals?" Alice asks and I shake my head. I pick them up. One is turquoise and sparkly, and the other is purple, and I love the energy I feel from it. When I pay, our hands brush and the hair on my arm stands up.

"Not really." I'm suddenly cold.

She gasps and drops my bag which clatters on the floor.

"Are you okay?" I pick up the bag.

She looks from Harry to me and for a second I think she recognises me. How can she, though?

"I've seen you." She points her finger at me.

"What do you mean?" I grasp Harry's hand tightly.

"You two. I've seen you. I've seen something. Are you together?" Her eyes flicker between us.

"Um, no," I stutter. What's with everyone?

"You need to sort it out. Stop going around in circles," she says, then disappears, leaving us baffled.

"Hello?" says a voice. I turn around and a man's standing where Alice was a minute ago. "I said is that everything?" He's waiting for me to answer him like I'm stupid.

"No, I'm..." My smile is fixed on my face as we walk away.

"What the fuck was that's all about?" Harry asks and I am shaking. I don't want to tell him what happened on New Year's Eve. How the fuck did that happen? How could Alice be here one minute and gone the next?

"Urm," Did he see Alice? "Can we have another drink?" I change the subject and we walk over to the mulled wine table.

❖ ❖ ❖

We sit down on a little bench just outside the church with the wind whipping around our faces.

"So, what the fuck happened in there?" Harry asks. I wonder why he is so interested.

Rog starts impatiently pulling on his lead and we start walking by the pier.

"Did you see the woman? She was standing by the crystals and then she was gone," I say and take a sip of my mulled wine. When we reach the pier, I let Rog off of his lead to sniff.

The sea looks cold but still and the clouds above

us are threatening rain.

Rog barks at the end of the pier. "Rog, no!" I shout, and Harry bends down to clip the lead onto him, but loses his balance and falls into the sea. Rog jumps in after and starts yapping.

"Fuck," Harry screams, thrashing around and swimming to the pier.

"Rog, get out," I say.

Harry throws the leash to me and I pull it to get him on the pier, but he yanks it and I fall into the sea. Harry jumps back in to get me out and whilst we are there, we just start laughing as our teeth chatter.

"It's fucking freezing," I screech, and pull myself and Harry up on the pier, Rog follows us, shaking all of the water off.

"Come here." Harry wraps his arms around me. I'm shivering, but I enjoy the warmth between us.

He silently helps me into the car whilst I shiver uncontrollably. Harry puts the heating on and I pull a blanket around me from the back of his car. Harry dries Rog and then sits down next to me.

"I'm sorry," he says and takes my hand, squeezing it.

"Harry it's fine," I say.

We look at each other, and I bite my lip. He leans forward and goes to put his arms around me. I start breathing heavily. Is this it? Is he going to kiss me properly this time? He doesn't. Instead, he seems to be looking for something. My stupid fucking heart.

◆ ◆ ◆

When we get back, Annie is alone. The sun is slowly going down over the mountains, even though it's late afternoon.

I let Rog into the cabin and then change my clothes.

I shake my head and cringe. Why would he keep leaning close to me if we aren't going to kiss? I am so frustrated and angry at myself for letting this happen. My head is more messed up than ever, and I am feeling sick and anxious.

"Where are Tammy and Razor?" I ask.

She nods towards their bedroom and shouts.

"Seriously, how long can you go on for?" Annie shouts from the living room.

I giggle.

Sometimes Tammy and Razor have days where you just don't see them. We often hang out together and sometimes they're just locked in their bedroom for days.

"So, why were you both out for so long?"

I don't know what to tell her. "We fell in the sea," I say eventually. At least that is the truth.

"Sure you did," she says, and rolls her eyes at us. "Well, I imagine your afternoon was more fun than mine."

I nod and sit down, careful not to interrupt her paintings that are sprawled out all over the room in different stages of being done.

"Am I the only sensible one here? Because I always thought I was the fucked up one?" she says.

"You are the sensible one," I say and she snorts.

"Come right into my studio, Harry," Annie says as Harry hovers around the door. "I might have to cancel this stupid grand opening." She says and sighs, looking at us.

"Can't you paint the mountains?" Harry suggests.

He brings over hot chocolate in mugs with whipped cream. I dread to think where that whipped cream has been.

"No cream for me, thanks. I know what the two of them do with it," Annie says and we smile.

We are silent whilst Annie studies us. I feel guilty even though we haven't done anything.

"So are you two…?" Annie's voice trails off and she sees the look on Harry's face. He looks horrified and I try to do the same expression. "Sorry, I was only asking." She shakes her head.

"Yeah well," Harry says. That sums everything up really.

"Why don't you take a break?" I ask, watching her get more frustrated with her paintings.

"Can we watch a film?" she asks.

We both nod and I open the cabinet with the TV inside.

"Your pick," I say, getting comfy on the sofa that pulls out to be a sofa bed. Harry flops down on the other side so our bare feet touch and a tingly sensation spread over me.

"I love *The Snowman*," she says. She is a high-powered businesswoman, but put her in front of *The Snowman* and she cries like a toddler.

I smile at Harry, while Annie is engrossed in the film, and think about this day. The view out of our window is gorgeous and with the fire crackling and the warmth of the room, I've never felt cosier. I pull the tartan blanket from behind me and it falls over our legs.

The rain patters softly on the window, and I don't know how Annie can't concentrate in this cabin.

◆ ◆ ◆

"Bloody hell; were you in a marathon sexathon?" Annie asks as the credits to *The Snowman* finish and Tammy emerges from her bedroom.

"We had some business to take care of." Tammy shrugs and jumps onto the other sofa.

"Business," I say and giggle.

"Did you get Christmas decorations?" Razor asks, looking around.

"No, we got drunk." Harry says while he winks at me.

I want to tell them about Mystic Alice. I especially want to tell Harry everything, but I'm so confused about what happened. Did she follow us?

"Right," Razor says. His raised eyebrow says it all.

CHAPTER 7

Connie drops off our tea: a steak and ale pie for us, and a smaller one for Rog, who wolfs it down. We eventually find some Christmas decorations in the loft.

Harry pulls a lever on the wall and some cute little steps unfold, leading to the attic. Is it safe? Fuck knows. Now, though, we're all in different states of drunkenness.

We stand at the top of the steps in the loft. Razor goes first and I'm behind Harry at the back with Rog darting between us, obviously excited to find a new place to sniff.

"Watch out for any loose planks," Harry whispers, and walks across the attic to the boxes in the corner.

It's dark except for a window in the corner that was more of a peephole.

"Don't touch anything," Tammy whispers as we gather around the boxes. A bookcase is in next to the window in the corner of the room. I shine my phone torch on it and see a few dusty books.

Harry kneels in front of the bookcase. I follow him and sit down on the floor.

"Coming?" Razor calls to us.

I look at Harry. "It's up to you if you want to have a look around," he says.

"I'll stay," I say to them, and Razor shrugs. I hear him disappear down the steps and the door closes. Rog is curled up next to the window.

"Look at these," Harry says, pulling out a couple of old-looking books.

"They look hundreds of years old." I run my hand over the slightly broken spine of the book. It smells musty and when I open it, it's flimsy and almost see-through.

A little envelope falls out of it.

"Look at the writing on this," Harry says.

"What's it written in?" It looks old and almost smudged. How long has all of this been here? How easily it could have been destroyed.

"Some kind of ink…" He runs his hand across the paper.

"Can you read it?" I look at the carefully swirling letters on the paper.

"It looks like some kind of contract." He squints to read it better.

"Do you know about the myths of Scotland?" he asks, and I shake my head. I love finding out about the history of places.

Harry passes the book and my eyes scan the page. I feel the tears in my eyes as I finish the last sentence. *How sad!*

"Em?" Harry scoots as close to me in the dark as he can. "Are you crying?" I let out a very impolite sniffle.

"It's so sad," I mumble, as the tears fall down my face.

"You daft cow. You know they are just myths. They might not be real." He takes my hand.

"But what if they are?" I whisper.

He strokes my hand with his, making my heart race again.

"If they are, then it's a sad tale, isn't it?" His voice is softer. I can't see his face in the darkness, and I'm quite glad he can't see mine.

"Em?" he says into the pitch-black attic.

"Yes," I whisper. His legs are pressed against mine and he still has my hand in his.

"Are you going to tell me what happened today?"

How do I tell him I rang the BBC drunk on New Year? How do I say the same woman was at that stall and then disappeared?

"Did you see the woman?" I ask.

"Yes," he replies.

"How did she just disappear?" I ask.

"I don't know. What was she talking about with the whole circle thing?" he asks.

"I don't know. Maybe that we've been through a lot together." I shrug.

We have, but we've already been going around in circles for years, starting with us dating each other, then being friends, and finally hating each other. Then repeat.

"Can you tell me the truth about something?" he asks.

Uh - oh.

The door opens, and a shadow stands on the stairs. The light behind them lit up the attic.

"Dudes, you up here?" Annie slurs.

"Yes," we answer.

"Hang on; you're decent, aren't you?" she asks.

"Yes," we repeat. I didn't realise Harry still has my hand. It feels normal.

"What are you doing up here?" she asks.

"Just reading," I say.

We carefully put the book back in the bookcase and, with our fingers still entwined; we walk carefully down the steps to the bright light of the lounge. Fuck knows how long we were up there. It's pitch black outside the window and I realise how hungry I am.

Rog follows us into the lounge where everyone is sitting.

"They aren't dead, guys," Annie shouts through the lounge.

"You both look like you've been up there for centuries." Tammy blows some dust off me and a cloud hazes my vision.

"We were just looking around." I say with a shrug.

If Harry doesn't want to tell them, then I'm not going to. It's kind of exciting that we're the only ones to find it.

"Just in time for pizza." Razor brings in four boxes of hot greasiness. Yes, this will go down a treat. Rog's ears cock up at the sign of pizza and he sits at our feet hoping to scrounge a runaway slice.

CHAPTER 8

For the rest of the evening, I feel something is weird between Harry and I. It's like we have rewound back to New Year. Maybe it's what we read tonight or how much time we've spent together. But I think I still feel something for him. Trouble is, it's too late.

I really want to go to the pools and the castle and see where everything happened. I'm not romantic. Far from it, I can't help but think of the myth and how sad it is. How much the chief and fairy loved each other.

When the others suggest drunken *Monopoly*, I just want to go to bed. Tomorrow is the light switch on in the village and I'm looking forward to it. What do the other villagers think of the myth? Should I ask around? I'm not sure why I feel so drawn to it.

◆ ◆ ◆

In bed that night, I snuggle close to Harry, enjoying being near him even though he is turned away from me. It's way too cold to sleep alone as the main fire is in the lounge and all the doors leave a tiny draft. Rog is snoring softly at the end of the bed.

Harry turns to me, his face breaking into a grin as soon as our eyes meet and I catch my breath.

"I'm freezing," I say shivering, even though I'm wearing my quilted, shapeless tartan Christmas pyjamas with a quilt and a blanket on top.

"Me too." He shuffles even closer, so I feel his breath on my face.

"Harry?"

He wraps his arms around me, and I stupidly wonder if he does this with Claire.

"Yeah?" he says.

"I want to go to the castle," I say excitedly.

"Then let's," he says, smiling. His eyes sparkle and my skin tingles all over.

***

"I want to let you all know Claire will be here tonight," Harry announces over breakfast.

"Great." Annie says and smiles.

"Yeah," I add. I don't know what I'm feeling, but I don't like it. I swirl my cereal around the spoon, then finally give up on it and dump it in the bin. Rog eats his breakfast next to the table.

"I was wondering if we can take her to the light switch on tonight," he says, looking around at us all.

When the locals talk about the light switch on, they make it sound like the event of the year.

Connie and Fergus are volunteering to help and so we are, too.

"Sure." Tammy says and takes a bite of her toast.

"It's going to be fandabidozi!" Annie says, waiting for her breakfast. My friends are honestly the biggest twats ever.

"Looking forward to it, Em?" Harry asks.

"Absolutely shitting myself with excitement," I reply sarcastically.

CHAPTER 9

The parade doesn't start until five pm, so at half past three, we leave the cabin dressed in our jackets and kitted from head to toe in warm hats and scarves. We even have a jacket and flashy collar for Rog. The weather looks unpredictable and the bitter wind has picked up from the morning.

We pile into the cars and Harry drives us into Portree. We arrive at the Inn Keeper and are immediately hit by the smell of stale beer and fire smoke.

It feels more like a home with a bar. All the rooms have beamed ceilings and fluorescent wall lights. The backroom has a brick fireplace that is lit up and crackling.

"Well, if the rest of the evening goes like this, I won't complain," Razor says, ordering four beers.

"You said it," Annie agrees and I nod.

The entire place feels welcoming, although I think we're early. The bar is practically empty, with just the owner cleaning the tables and a few people playing snooker.

One of the local villagers walks in with half the

village behind him. They are all wearing hi-vis jackets.

The youngest one of the group spots us and comes over.

"I've not seen you around," he says, introducing himself as Peter.

"We are just here for Christmas," Razor says and introduces us all.

"You're one of us, then?" he says, noticing Razor's accent.

He shakes hands with all of us and pats Rog on the head.

"Santa's helpers, can you all gather here for your outfits?" a lady called Ellen says. We're given costumes to change into. Everyone is waving their arms around and getting changed into their outfits. I'm an angel. I get given a sheet and a halo to wear. This isn't going to keep me warm.

"You make a cute angel," Harry whispers, not loud enough for anyone to hear but me.

"What are you dressing as?" I ask.

"I'm going to be an ass," he says, shoving himself into the back end of a donkey.

Tammy reluctantly comes over to put the other half on and I laugh more than I probably should.

"Ranulph, darling." Connie comes in dressed from head to toe as Mrs Claus while Fergus is Santa.

"Kill me now, please," Razor whispers to me and I giggle.

"Do you want to be our elf?" Connie asks, showing him the elf outfit with stripy leggings, a red waistcoat and a bow.

"Not really Ma, if I'm honest," he says. Connie tuts, disappointed.

"Now, loveys, get this down your pipe holes," Nancy says, bringing over a tray of shots.

"A drop of whisky has never hurt anyone." She says and winks.

The locals around here are so friendly that I feel right at home.

"I want to be so bladdered I don't remember any of this," I say.

"I second that," Razor says from the table. Harry and Tammy have been guided away and briefed.

Annie is dressed in a mini, red, frilly elf dress with striped tights to match Razor's leggings. Someone has put little bells on Rog, so he jingles when he walks.

"Here are your wings, little angel." Someone comes over and attaches wings to me and they're massive. I feel like I am going to clip someone around the head with them whenever I move.

"Now I've been told to brief you on what's happening. You won't be flying very high, but we are going to attach this rope to you."

Hang on, what?

They weren't kidding; they attach a small harness to me.

"Don't worry, love." Connie pats me on the back.

"Don't worry kiddo; you're only going from here

to here," Ellen says as if that makes me feel better.

❖ ❖ ❖

My stomach knots and I feel sick, but we head outside into the cold and darkness. A car with a sleigh on it is already parked in front of the Inn Keeper, blasting out 'Wonderful Christmas Time' by Paul McCartney. The crowds have already gathered in the carpark opposite and are lining the streets as far as I can see. Everyone has deer antlers on and Santa hats.

We get quickly briefed on our route. And I make sure I have another shot of whisky before we leave.

We start walking in a line, holding tightly to Rog on his lead. Annie and Razor are naturals, waving at the crowds that have whistles. It's cute seeing the sparkle in the kids' eyes when we walk by. Santa has a microphone and is talking to the crowds.

We weave around Bank Street and up the hill. The crowds follow slowly behind us. Harry is panting under the costume, even in the cold air that's now like swords cutting into any exposed skin.

The sky feels like it is getting darker by the minute, but we all dance to the Christmas songs blasting from the car.

I am so hot in my costume, with my coat underneath; I look like a very chubby angel.

"Not long to go, I hope," Annie whispers.

"I hope not," I whisper back. I should have worn better shoes than these dolly pumps. My feet are killing me with every movement.

We stop when we reach what looks like a farm.

"Ladies and gentlemen, the moment you've been waiting for. Come Dasher, come Dancer, come Prancer, come Vixen. On Comet, on Cupid, on Donner, on Blitzen!"

The reindeer appear attached to handlers dressed as elves. Rog starts barking and trying to pull towards them, but I tighten his lead. The handlers give Annie and Razor the rope and; I have to admit, I'm a little scared. They're bloody massive.

We carry on walking down the hill and past the harbour that's next to the church.

"Welcome to the Portree light switch on. My name is Glenda," the lady at the front of the church, standing on a little platform, says. The church is full of villagers waiting for us to arrive. A drinks table is positioned in the corner, laden with jugs of juice and what looks like mulled wine. A little girl on the stage is wearing a costume similar to mine and starts singing about the angel. Glenda comes over to me.

"Now, lovey, you're going to go fly onto the stage from here, and don't worry, it's a bungee jump." She hands me a bag of sweets to 'scatter,' to the children on my way.

More children join the angel on the stage and they start singing 'Little Donkey'.

Tammy and Harry smile and make their way onto the stage, knocking into the crowds and apologising. I giggle, feeling slightly tipsy. They finally make it up and I'm signalled to go. The children are fussing Rog, so I leave his lead and get ready.

I take a giant leap as Glenda told me to do and bounce on my harness, through the crowd, crash landing straight into the donkey and knocking Harry and Annie flying.

"I'm so sorry," I say, standing up, feeling slightly dizzy. My halo slips and I readjust it onto my head.

I help them both up. Tammy lets go of my hand, but Harry holds on.

"Are you okay?" he whispers.

My hands are shaking and my knees are doing the bloody 'Bend and Snap' and I fear he is going to try to kiss me. Thank God I didn't do a *Bridget Jones* and expose my knickers.

"I think so," I say. He squeezes my hand, and the crowd erupts into applause. Glenda is beaming at us proudly.

"Kiss her, kiss her." The crowd starts chanting. I don't want to steal the thunder from the kids, but they seem happy enough. Harry shrugs and holds me close to him. I can smell the beer on his breath. We are both way too drunk as we lean in so our lips are almost touching. My lips are shaking like the rest of me, and I close my eyes. A screechy noise breaks out from the back.

"What the actual fuckery is this?" We break

apart and turn around to see Claire standing by the door. *Oh fuck.*

CHAPTER 10

The light switch on is kind of boring after 'Claire bear' arrives.

Harry's purposely avoiding me and all the knots are back in my stomach. Glenda and Santa are standing in the middle of the village where the Christmas tree towers over the smaller buildings. Glenda counts down and then plugs in the lights. The Christmas tree is aglow with different coloured bulbs. The lamp posts dotted around the streets are also lit up and twinkling in the moon.

When we all go to the Inn Keeper pub, I'm left at the lonely singles table.

"This right here." Annie gestures toward me. "Is why I don't do relationships," she says.

"I am the biggest fucking moron in the world," I say.

I lay my head in my hands and hope I wake up in the cabin and this is a really bad dream. I've had too much to drink, and watching Harry and Claire awkwardly shuffle is making me feel sick. Rog is obediently lying on my feet, keeping them warm. I'm thankful for him at least. The only decent man

I have in my life.

"I thought that was it," Annie cuts through my pity-thinking and puts her arm on mine; I know she understands.

"Mm," I say and cringe when I think about the entire town knowing my business.

"She should be the one getting drunk on her own." Annie's voice has a hint of venom in it.

Razor and Tammy sit down beside us.

"Sorry Em." Tammy squeezes my shoulders.

"I'm going home," I announce.

"No, don't let that twat ruin your night," Annie says, and Tammy nods.

"I just want to go home," I sigh. I look up, although my vision is slightly clouded, and Mystic Alice is sitting opposite me. Her lips are pursed together and she's watching me. Twice now, I've embarrassed myself in front of this woman. She's so strange though, sat all on her own.

"I want to move my things out of their bedroom," I say. My throat thickens and my eyes tear up.

"Get this down your neck." Nancy comes over to sit with us and puts her arms around my shoulders. "This will make you forget all your problems." She winks.

Glenda and her husband Joe also sit down at our table, which is slowly being surrounded by the locals. I recognise a few of them, but can't remember all their names. Annie is happily chatting up Peter.

"You don't need a man. You're still young," Joe says over the table.

"If you kiss a few toads, eventually you'll get your prince," Glenda says.

I cringe at that. I don't want any toads or princes. This isn't some fairy-tale bullshit. I bite my tongue and hold my glass up when everyone toasts to good health. I can't help my eyes slowly watching Harry and Claire, who are now cuddling by the fire.

"Well sweetheart, do you know the myth of Skye?" Glenda whispers

I nod. "A little."

"The fairies of Skye," she continues.

"I have read something about a chief and fairy," I say.

The book in the attic springs to mind. I think about how happy I was when I was there.

"That's the one. Well, word is, after all of that happened, the fairies kept guard of the island and strange things happen here when you are in love," she says.

I cringe at the word *love*. *I don't love him, do I?* I don't know what I feel now except incredibly drunk and embarrassed.

"Now Glenn, don't be telling nonsense ghost stories. You'll scare the poor girl." Joe winks.

"It's true Dad," Peter chips in after he and Annie join us again.

"Of course it is. The fairies have helped all of us," pipes in Hannah, who runs the little café on the corner.

"We've all been married for years. You can't say that's not a coincidence." Glenda's eyes sparkle as she drinks her wine.

"So the fairies are pairing everyone off?" I ask, feeling stupid again.

"That's right," Peter says.

"That's romantic," Annie adds.

"It is." Peter nods.

"But how do they pair you up with the right person?" I ask.

"Well, that's the thing, love. Have you heard about the Fairy Pools near to here?" she asks.

"Those Fairy Pools are more trouble than they're worth." Nancy chips into the conversation while doing her rounds.

"Glenda, love, it's a myth, remember?" Joe says and shakes his head.

"Never say never," she says, smiling.

"You know he believed it once," she adds in a whisper.

Am I in a town of looneys? Fuck knows. Do I believe fairies watch over the island and bring people together? Maybe. But I've drunk a little too much.

"Do you believe it?" Annie asks me. She's beyond drunk now - if that's a thing. Tammy and Razor help her to their car.

"Can I come?" I ask.

Can't they hear me? Or do they just hate me? The car pulls out and I'm left to go home with... Oh, God. No.

❖ ❖ ❖

I'm stuck in the fucking car with Claire and Harry and they're being disgustingly soppy. I blame the radio spouting out power ballads at this time of night.

"My schmooze woozy." Claire marks her territory, after giving me sly side looks through the mirror. I just want to go to bed, or the sofa, or wherever I'm sleeping.

She fluffs up his hair, and he pushes her hand off of him. I feel like I'm watching someone completely different and not the best friend I've known forever.

"My Clairy beary," he says, and she sits back, grinning like the cat that got the cream.

We finally get back to the cabin and I walk ahead of them with Rog so I don't have to see them be lovey. They're sickening.

"We are home," I drunkenly shout through the cabin. Rog immediately marks his spot on the sofa.

"Let's go to bed, baby," Claire says.

I don't want to bring up where I'm sleeping, so I loudly drag my bags across the floor.

"I guess I won't need this room tonight, schmooze woozy," I say and grin. I know they're watching me and I'm secretly happy she knows we've been sleeping together.

"Come on, Rog," I call to him and he follows me into Annie's bedroom, where I settle down in my makeshift bed.

"What do you mean, you shared a room? What does that mean?" I can hear her shrieking.

CHAPTER 11

I sleep restlessly and, on top of that, I'm cold. I just want to stay in bed and nurse this hangover.

"Bitches, breakfast," Tammy shouts from the hallway.

Annie is snoring in her bed next to me.

"Come on Em," she shouts.

"They aren't awake yet." Razor whispers.

I wrap my dressing gown around myself and walk into the kitchen. The log fire crackles in the lounge. Razor lets Rog out into the garden for a wee.

"Coffee?" Tammy sets out breakfast on the table. There are plates of crumpets and pancakes, toast and something potatoey I don't recognise. If I'm honest, it's turning my stomach.

"Do you want to talk about it?" Tammy asks, picking apart her toast. Tammy doesn't eat the crust.

"No," I say and shake my head which feels like a drummer is hitting it as hard as they can.

"It isn't that bad. That boy needs a good shake, though," Razor says.

"Every time you break up we are devastated for you both," Tammy says.

They know how we've both felt, over the years. Well, I still do. But I'm so confused.

"Why can't you just be straightforward about it all?" Razor asks.

"I mean, they almost kissed. How much more proof do you need?" Tammy asks.

"Except he has a girlfriend," I say.

"But he wouldn't have nearly kissed you if he didn't want to," Tammy says, holding her hands up.

Harry walks in and I tense up.

"God, dude, what are you wearing?" Razor asks.

"Annie is going to have a field day with you," Tammy replies.

I look at him in his grey tweed suit. His hair is brushed neatly. I'm guessing Claire has done this. He looks like a right twat.

"Tweed," he replies, tucking into some toast.

I don't know what to say to him, but the tension in the room is making me uncomfortable and I feel sicker than I did before. Tammy hands me two paracetamol and I neck them along with the coffee she made me.

"Morning," Harry says to me with a smile and I feel a little sadder. Today could have been so different if Claire hadn't disrupted us.

"Morning," I say as casually as I can. Has he forgotten what happened last night? Or has he erased it because he doesn't feel the same way?

Snow Barbie walks in wearing furry-heeled boots and a thick fuchsia pink jumper.

"Why do you stay here? It's freezing," she says, shivering for emphasis. The night wind has died down, and the ground is covered in sparkly frost.

"Go and sit by the fire," Razor says. Tammy rolls her eyes and I cough to hide my laughter. Where did she think she was going to? Fucking California?

"Thank you." Claire ignores us and goes to sit by the fire. Razor makes us a huge mug of hot chocolate overflowing with cream and sprinkles.

"Thank you," I say graciously, licking the cream and getting it on my nose.

"I'd better go and sit with her." Harry takes the rest of his breakfast and walks to the fireplace.

"She is settling in well," Tammy whispers.

"Annie is going to rip them both to shreds," I say.

"At least he doesn't look happy," Tammy whispers.

It's weirdly true, and I never noticed it before. He acts different around Claire. Is he actually in love?

He quickly wipes the crumbs off his jacket.

I eat the rest in silence. If only a lot of things had been different. I bet the fairies didn't have this problem.

❖ ❖ ❖

"Hello? Is it us you're looking for?" Connie and Fergus come in singing from the hallway.

"Is everyone decent?" Connie covers her eyes. I love Razor's parents and the fact Razor cringes when they're near.

"Yes, we are." Razor offers them breakfast.

"It's alright, boy, we've had our breakfast," Fergus says. Harry appears in the doorway and says hello.

"Ah, now you're all here. I just want to tell you about the events of today at the Fairy Pools. The pools themselves are breath-taking," Connie says. Her eyes twinkle and Fergus takes her hand.

I pick up the leaflet. The pictures on the front look stunning.

"Urm, I can't," Razor says quickly.

"I want to go shopping today," Claire says. I sense Harry reading the leaflet over my shoulder.

"Wow," Harry says.

"Baby, I thought you were coming shopping," Claire whines. I let Harry take the leaflet.

"Fairies," he whispers. We must be thinking about the same thing. The fairy myth from the books. Everyone seems to believe it. Does it come from here? My curiosity piques and Harry's smile says he feels the same.

"Yes, lovey, why don't you go?" Connie says.

"It's a popular tourist spot," Fergus says.

"Won't it be cold?" I ask.

"It's magic, love, of course not." Connie winks,

and I feel a surge of excitement. I want to see it all.

"You're not serious, are you?" Claire appears, and the magic disappears. Even though I am tingling with anticipation, Claire's voice breaks whatever is going on between us.

"Yes," I say.

I go off to get ready. If he isn't coming, then I can still have fun. I can see the history of the pools. I don't need him.

"Its history," Harry says, and I hear the disappointment in his voice.

"Some disgusting-looking pool?" Claire asks. I bite my lip and Connie and Fergus smile, although it looks fake.

"Don't mock it till you try," Fergus says. Tammy and Razor leave. I don't hear what Razor says to Harry, but he freezes.

"Harry, baby, you promised you would come shopping." Claire pouts.

I'm a fool. I shouldn't feel the way I do.

I go out to the off-road car. My vision clouds as I start it up. The tears I've felt since last night finally fall. I don't want to be crying again. Do I love Harry? I'm not sure if it's love or wanting someone I can't have. I'm so fed up of feeling like this.

CHAPTER 12

The window is wound down even though it's cold, but mostly for Rog. Will the pool be cold? Fuck knows. Will I go in? Again, I don't know, but I want to see it.

The air is crisp, and the road is bumpy. The countryside stretches for miles.

Why isn't anyone else here?

Well, I know why Harry isn't but Tammy and Razor could see his family anytime.

I cringe, thinking about how it looks, me being here on my own. I'm the single girl who got rejected in front of strangers. My eyes cloud up and the tears come. I have to stop the car. I'm not sure why I'm crying. Do I feel alone? What do I want out of my life? Am I crying because it's too late? I shake my head, angry with myself.

My phone buzzes next to me.

I'm sorry we can't get rid of her. Have fun x. Tam.

Anger surges through me as the tears continue. I shouldn't have to fight to spend time with my friend. Everything seems so awkward between us since we nearly kissed. It's quite obvious he regrets it.

I pull into the stony car park and get out, holding the lead. There are a few cars dotted around, and I spot Glenda heading towards me.

"Emilia, love."

"Hi," I say and smile at her.

"Oh dear, is that man of yours making you cry?"

I must have puffy red eyes. Damn you, Harry.

"He should be here too," she says.

I shrug and look around, breathing in the slightly moist air as it starts to drizzle.

As Glenda walks back to her car, I pull out the rucksack Connie packed for me and head along the path.

A little stone path winds along the edge of the grassy mountainside. How beautiful it must look with the wildflowers in the summer.

The bottom of the mountains is split in half by a bubbling stream. I step across the river to reach the top of the Fairy Pools.

I look around and it feels like the middle of nowhere. What if I get lost? Are there wild animals here? How long would it take for me to be found?

◆ ◆ ◆

I stop near the edge, listening to the water flowing underneath me, and peer over the edge. The most beautiful waterfall flows into a steep pool that's all different shades of green and blue.

I sit on the edge and take off my rucksack.

Rog sniffs around the rocks next to me. My face is slightly damp from the drizzle and spray from the waterfall. This is it. This is the most beautiful thing I've ever seen. A lump rises in my throat. I've never cried this much and here I am crying over water.

The drizzle turns into a light downpour and I know I'm going to get cold out here, but I want to stay no matter what the weather is. I'm going to get into the water. The cold air whips around my bare feet as I shuffle close to the edge.

The air here is so different and fresh compared to back home. I've never been a nature lover, but I suddenly feel full of energy.

"Em?" the voice behind me sounds alarming. Am I going mad and hearing Harry in my head? I need to tune him out and focus on the flowing water. It's so peaceful.

Footsteps crunch under the rocks behind me and a shadow looms over me. Rog starts barking and growling until Harry bends down to fuss him.

"Fuck's sake, Em, you scared me." Harry sits next to me and when I open my eyes, he's no longer wearing tweed. He's changed into a light grey raincoat and his hair looks normal.

"Why?" I ask, wondering if Claire is here.

"You haven't been answering your phone and then I got a text saying come here," he says.

My phone has been in my bag and if I am honest, I haven't even looked at it since I arrived.

"I haven't sent any texts," I say.

The air between us is awkward. This is my best friend who I've known forever and I don't know what to say to him.

"Look down," I say, changing the subject and he does. His eyes sparkle and he grins at me. My whole body tingles.

"Are you getting in?" he asks.

"Yes," I say. I take off my coat and throw it on top of my bag. I strip down until I am in my pants and a t-shirt. Harry does the same. The wind makes me shiver.

"So you didn't text me? he asks.

"No," I say and shake my head.

"I left my phone in my bag," I say.

I look down, wondering why exactly he's here. I'm a little sad that he hasn't come because he wants to.

"It was the fairies," he says, lightening the tone.

"You sound worse than the locals," I say. He laughs a good hearty laugh. I miss spending time with him.

He splashes me, and the water is freezing. I let out a yelp.

"Harry!" I squeal and he laughs.

"It was the fairies," he repeats.

I giggle. Bloody fairies.

"In all honesty, though, isn't this place incredible?" I say with a sigh, looking around.

"It is," he whispers.

I am a fool for believing everyone. There isn't

another person here at all. There isn't an event going on at all. How has this happened and why is Harry here?

The mountains are a blur in the distance thanks to the rain, and it's cold, but adrenaline is keeping me warm. Being next to Harry like this is thrilling, but I can't help noticing the awkwardness between us.

"Do you believe the myth?" I ask as we sit above the pool, dangling our feet over the edge. Our legs are side by side and touching.

"What? That a love fairy has match made everybody in the village?"

"Everyone seems pretty sure of it."

"I believe there was something magical in this place, but I feel over the generations and centuries it's been twisted into a love story. Maybe the villagers are together for so long because they love each other, but I don't think the pool or fairies have anything to do with it." He looks at me seriously.

"I think it's real," I say enthusiastically. I don't realise I believe it until I say it out loud.

"Well, everyone has to believe in something to keep them sane," Harry says, standing up. "I should get back."

"Does Claire know you've come?" I ask.

"No," he answers. His voice breaks. What is he thinking?

CHAPTER 13

I am shivering as we make our way back to Portree. Tammy and Razor are at the Inn Keeper, but I want to get warm and comfortable in my PJs and watch a film.

The centre of the square is crowded with locals and tourists. Harry drives in circles until he finds a parking space in the pub.

We walk across the gravel and through the crowds to find our friends near the front of the square. Harry leaves to find Claire.

"Em." Tammy waves me over. She's standing with Annie and Razor.

"Where in the world of *Narnia* have you been?" Annie demands, pointing a gloved finger at me.

It's still cold and I'm still a little wet. Luckily the rain from this morning has died down.

Glenda stands in the centre of the square on a platform in front of the microphone. A few members of the council committee are with her.

"Hello, Portree. I want to welcome you to our annual Wishing Tree event. To the villagers, new and old, here is what we do. Everybody picks up a little hanging note, you write your wish on it, and hang it on our village tree," she shouts through the microphone.

Villagers line up under the towering tree for miles.

"This is some soppy shit," Annie slurs.

Annie doesn't do true love. Its physical attraction or nothing to her, and the way Peter is hanging around her, she has him right where she wants him.

Razor and Tammy are at the front, writing their wishes.

We all move up the line and I realise I'm standing next to Harry. Being this close to him makes me hold my breath.

"Hi." I exhale sharply

"Hey," he says, his hands in his pockets, shuffling his feet. Why is it so awkward between us?

I cringe at the atmosphere.

We arrive at the front and both simultaneously pick up a golden envelope and a pen.

I watch him frown and scribble on his, then cross it out and rewrite something, then seal it. He looks a little pink.

What should I write? I bite the end of my pen. *I love him.*

I sigh, knowing it's true, but feeling my cheeks scorch. Harry is watching me. I fucking love Harry Birchwood and there isn't a thing I can do about it.

My stomach is throbbing as I write it on my paper. I've finally admitted what I've been trying to hide.

What did he write and rewrite?

"Here you are." Princess Barbie finds us as soon as we get away from the crowd.

Harry seems jumpy. She grips his hand like he's about to blow away.

"Yes, I'm here," he says finally.

I attach my wish, thinking about what Harry wrote. I cringe when I think of anyone reading mine. Thank God I didn't write my name on it.

"Did you wish for the perfect girlfriend to love you?" she asks in the same voice I use for Rog. Harry looks flustered.

"Damn, you got me," he says with a smile, and I bite my lip to stop myself from laughing. The sarcasm is lost on her.

"You don't need to wish for me, baby, I'm here." She squeezes his cheeks and I stifle my laughter with a cough. She's insufferable.

***

I walk over to where my friends are sitting at the Inn Keeper after we have finished our notes. Rog takes his spot by my feet.

"She is awful!" Annie whispers to me, while Peter has his arms all over her.

"Mhm," I say. I didn't want to bitch, but how can he not see it?

"Are you okay?" she asks. I nod, downing my drink.

"Amazing," I reply sarcastically.

Harry joins us with Claire still clinging to his hand.

"Harry mate, fancy a game of darts?" Razor gets up.

"Sure." He goes to stand up, but Claire scowls at him.

"But, Harry, baby, I want a kiss." She purses her lips. Harry reluctantly kisses her. I look away.

"Me too, Harry baby," Annie teases.

"And me." Tammy says and giggles.

I order another drink when Nancy comes over.

"It's freezing in this fucking place," Claire whines.

"Mate, you came to Scotland at Christmas. What did you expect?" Annie asks.

"Well, when we go on holiday it's always somewhere warm," she says snottily.

Razor comes back for his pint before going back to Harry.

"Girls, I think Razor is going to propose," Tammy whispers when Razor is out of sight.

Annie and I squeal.

"He doesn't know I'm on to him," she whispers.

"So why do you think he will?" Claire asks.

Oh, right, I forgot she was still here and sticking her nose into conversations that don't concern her.

"Because I know him well," she says, clearly flustered.

"Razor was acting "dodgy" outside the old jewellers," Annie pipes in.

"Oh, Tam, that's amazing." I squeal.

Claire doesn't look impressed.

"Is that what you wished for under the tree?" I ask.

She nods guiltily. "I know they say it's a myth, but it's so romantic." Her voice is barely a whisper.

"Oh God, you don't believe that absolute nonsense, do you?" Claire scoffs.

"Yes," I say at the same time as Tammy.

All the villagers that have made us feel so welcome. It's hard not to feel the magic, and I felt it this morning at the pools.

"Oh, please," she says and rolls her eyes.

"If it makes you feel less stupid, I wished for inspiration for my painting," Annie adds.

I giggle at Annie's participation in the group discussion.

"What's going on?" Harry comes back over and Claire grips his hand. He looks at her, confused.

"Why don't you tell them your news, baby cakes?" she says and I feel sick in my mouth. *Oh God, what news?*

"Um, are you sure?" he asks, looking away from us all.

We all wait, staring at them. "We're moving in together," Harry says finally.

"You're moving in together?" Tammy repeats his words.

"Yes, but that isn't all. We are moving to Birmingham. To be closer to daddy." Claire looks thrilled and Harry smiles at her.

I have an out-of-body experience. Like I am

watching all of this from above. My mind is numb and I don't know how I feel about my best friend moving away.

"But why?" Razor asks.

"Because it beats being a sad and lonely almost thirty-year-old," Harry says.

"Daddy has offered Harry a bigger position at the bank." Claire says, clearly ignoring Harry.

I think about what Harry has said. Does he want to move away? He wouldn't be lonely. My heart aches for what could have been.

"I think it's a cause for celebration." Claire beckons Nancy over, who doesn't look happy.

"What can I get you?" she asks.

"Do you do cocktails?" she asks.

"No, lovey, the best we can do is a slightly posher wine," she says and smiles at Claire, who decides what she wants.

"So you're leaving?" Tammy asks.

"Yes," Harry answers curtly.

"Well, good luck to you, mate." Razor clicks everyone's glasses. I join in, though I am still in a daze. I don't think my head has quite caught up with what all of this means. I'm losing my best friend.

"So will you still be available for piss ups or will it be fine caviar and cocktails from now on?" Annie mocks. Harry looks at Claire and I raise my eyebrow. He shouldn't have to ask.

"Of course," Claire says brightly, squeezing his hand.

"I don't feel so good," I lie, and gather all of my stuff together. Tammy and Annie beg me to stay, but there's only one place I want to be.

CHAPTER 14

I sit cross-legged in the musty attic with a glass of cheap wine, reading through the books in the bookcase. Rog has ditched me and chosen to sit with the others.

I flick through the history books and sigh. There are so many paintings of fairies in books from villager interpretations. The village believes the myth.

'If the myth is true, why is my love life still so shit?' I whisper out loud.

I hear footsteps.

"Em?" A shadow appears at the top of the attic door. My eyes adjust to the darkness and I see Harry.

I wipe my eyes, frustrated by the tears threatening to fall. Luckily, the light is dim enough to hide them.

"Shouldn't you be packing?" I whisper sarcastically.

"We aren't leaving until Boxing Day," he says.

I ignore him and flick through the Christmas Tree Tradition.

This attic feels like a magical cave with secret

books leading to a different world. Every different book I read, I get more excited about the history of the island.

Knowing it is just me and Harry is exciting too, like we've escaped into a magical world of fairies.

He plonks himself down next to me and I sniff the air. "Oh God, what are you wearing?" I choke.

The air next to me fills up with strong- smelling aftershave.

"Claire bought it for me."

"Harry, you have changed since you've been with her."

I flick through the pictures of the Christmas tree over the years. The picture right now is from the nineteen-twenties. The trees were decorated in ribbon and satin.

Harry ignores me and reads over my shoulder. Our hands touch as he skims the page.

"Wow," he says.

I have to admit, it's pretty amazing. As we turn the pages, the decades go by and the trees appear taller with plastic and glass decorations.

"It's incredible." I swallow a lump in my throat.

"The history is incredible," he says with a sigh.

I bet he sits with Claire talking about designer gloves. Wow, I sound petty.

He shuffles closer and our arms and legs are touching. I wonder if he still feels anything for me. Has he completely got over what we used to be and is ready to live in a giant mansion with Claire?

We reach the last page with a blank space that I

guess is for this year, and we both touch the page delicately.

"Em, you know I'm not going to Australia. You'll see me all the time," Harry starts.

"Are you happy?" I ask impulsively. I sound like a therapist.

Did he just gulp? I'm sure I've just heard him gulp.

"Yes. I am finally in an adult relationship I might actually be able to keep and I won't end up a sad and depressed old man," he says. I flinch.

He moves away from me and I can sense the tension between us. It's just as awkward as it was at the Fairy Pools.

"I don't like what this holiday has done to us," I say eventually. My cheeks feel warm. Thank God it's dark.

"I know," he admits. What is running through his head right now?

"We need to talk about it," I say.

❖ ❖ ❖

The dim light flickers, making us jump, and Harry knocks over my glass. We're both breathless as he turns on his torchlight and shines it around.

The wine glass is lying on its side, the contents spilling under the bookshelf.

"Shit," we say and find an old cloth to mop it up.

Slightly dazed, we look at each other through the glow of the phone torch. I don't know what to say, but my stomach is knotted and I'm trying not to think too much. Harry touches his hair awkwardly.

"Sorry," he says eventually.

He shuffles up next to me again.

I open the book back at the empty page that now has wine spilt in it.

"Oh, shit," I say.

He looks at me and I start panicking. My breathing is out of control and my eyes well up again.

"Don't cry," he says, taking one of my hands. I can't help the tightening of the knots in my stomach. Today has been shit, and I'm completely overwhelmed by my feelings.

"Em?" He turns off the torch and we're plunged into darkness.

"I've ruined it," I squeak.

"It was a blank page," he says.

We hear voices and Claire shouts for Harry.

"I should probably go. I'm sorry…" He stumbles and heads for the door.

I nod, still crying. Stupid books and stupid fairies.

I had planned to stay here all night, but now the light has gone and Harry is climbing downstairs.

I feel more alone than I've ever felt in my life. I think I got carried away by the Fairy Pools and the Christmas tree.

If Razor proposes, and Harry and Claire move in together, then our friendships are over and Harry, despite what he says, won't visit. It'll just be Annie and me. When Annie and Peter start their lives together, I'll be the last single friend. The sad loser they'll all be wary of telling anything to in case they upset me.

The trap door opens again and Harry throws a bundle of blankets and a couple of pillows at me. "Hey," I yell. I pick up my phone and flash the torch at the door. Harry is standing there.

"Thought you might be cold." He shrugs but smiles at me.

"Thank you," I say.

I arrange them into a bed. I know I'll be more comfortable up here than on the floor in Annie's room, and at least I can't hear anyone having sex.

Harry sits at the bottom of my bed.

"Want company?" he asks, and I open the quilt for him. My head screams for me to tell him to go away, but my heart can't deal with that thought.

"I can't leave without saying I'm sorry for not telling you," he says.

"I don't get why you didn't. You've been funny with me this whole trip," I say.

He draws in a sharp breath.

"Harry, you've changed so much this last month. I feel like I don't know you any more," I add.

I'm on a roll to piss off my friend.

"I've grown up, Em. I've realised that what we had is childish. Don't you worry about being left alone?"

"I wasn't alone," I say, the tears filling my eyes.

Were we childish? Did he ever love me?

"You can't be with someone because you're worried about being alone."

"Don't you think it's time we moved on? Me and you, we've tried all of this. We can't make it work. I have the chance to live a pretty amazing life with a brand new start. If it was you, I'd be encouraging it."

Oh God, don't cry again, I tell myself, but I can't help it.

I don't let out any noise; instead, I bite my lip. If the tables were turned and I was moving in with someone else, would he be happy for me? We'll never know because that isn't the situation.

"Would you?" I ask. I wanted to add if he realises being lonely isn't a reason to stay with someone.

"Of course," he says matter-of-factly.

I turn around so I'm facing him and lie down on the cushion that looks like it's seen better days.

"Won't Claire wonder where you've gone?" I ask.

"Maybe." He shrugs. Like he doesn't want to talk about her.

"See what I mean? You are being weird."

"Em, Claire doesn't like us being friends."

"So, are you moving because you love her or because you are scared of being alone?"

"Because I love her," he says.

We sit in silence whilst I think about everything and realise I won't be getting any sleep. Harry shuffles around, then sighs.

In my head, I'm telling him I love him and we'll run to each other. Is this a daydream, or have I fallen asleep?

CHAPTER 15

My clock shows seven am, and the moon is shining out of the tiny window in the attic. Harry snores on the chair beside me.

My heart flutters when I realise he stayed with me all night and nothing happened.

The attic is pitch black and the books we were looking at rest on the table. I think about the Christmas tree book and how we nearly ruined it. I also think about the Christmas tree of wishes and how stupid I was to put my true feelings on my piece of paper. Can I sneak it back and get rid of it before anyone sees it? Could I sneak a look at Harry's note at the same time?

Harry stirs next to me. "Em?" He looks up, surprised. Rog is at the end of the bed sleeping.

"Yes." I wrap the blanket around me. I have a few texts from Tammy and Annie from last night.

OMG Em! You just left me, man. Not cool -
Annie x
Are you okay, babe? Tam.

I look up at Harry, who's rubbing his eyes. It's freezing, but we must have huddled together at some point. The thought sends sparkly chills through me.

"We should probably go downstairs," he says, pulling on his dressing gown.

"Yeah," I agree. I can't help but feel disappointed.

He doesn't look at me once as he gets ready and walks down the ladder.

I swallow the lump in my throat and follow him.

"Is there an attic full of money that you've found?" Annie asks sleepily.

She's wearing a lacy nightie, and I wonder if Peter's here.

"Sure," I say and smile. *I wish.*

"So, no progress?" she asks. "He hasn't asked you to marry him?"

Harry comes into the kitchen with Claire.

"Morning," Annie says and pulls a face behind their backs. I bite my lip and turn back to my cup of coffee. I'm not hungry. I am a little nauseous. I serve up Rog's breakfast.

"Good morning, Emilia," Claire says and smiles. Harry nods at me.

"Hi Em," he says casually.

I join Annie with her enormous bowl of Cornflakes.

"Where's Tam and Razor?" I ask. The table is quiet with just us four. It's so bloody awkward too.

"They slept over at Razor's parents," she says.

"We were going to join their party, weren't we, baby?" Claire smiles at Harry.

"Yeah, we were," he says.

"Great," I say.

"Too busy with all your little fairies?" She sneers.

"Well, I think it's all romantic." Annie has gone all starry-eyed and gooey. Lucky for her, she has Peter.

"It is, and it isn't just fairies, it's history." I glare. She's mocking something that goes back centuries.

"Yuck," she says.

I exchange glances with Annie.

"I think it's interesting," Harry interjects.

"The man can speak then," I say sarcastically. He stares at me.

"Maybe he doesn't want to speak to you," Claire says to me.

"God, we aren't going to have this all day, are we? It's Christmas, guys," Annie interrupts.

It's a shame I don't have anything planned. Maybe I'll go back up to the attic and read more history, or go to the castle where the fairy cloth is. The thought of the myth makes me feel warm.

"So are you coming carolling tonight?" Annie asks.

"Urn," I start.

She's having none of it.

"Please, Em." She bats her eyelashes at me.

"Okay." I sigh. She hugs me, shouting in my ear to meet her here so we can get ready together.

"Oh, it's a shame we can't go carolling, isn't it, baby?" Claire's sickly voice shrills.

"Why?" he asks. I shouldn't eavesdrop. But here I am by the door, holding my breath and listening.

Annie crouches down next to me.

"Anything juicy?" she quizzes me. I bat her away.

"By the way, I read over your shoulder what your wish was." I watch her face for any signs of a joke, but she's deadly serious.

"Please tell him before he moves in with Elle Woods meets Barbie," she pleads. I giggle.

"I can't." I sigh.

It was a year ago we got together again. Just after the party with my parents when we slept together and talked through the whole night about our dreams. I told him I wanted him to do something for me. I didn't know what yet, but I felt like I could tell him anything.

How the tables have turned.

I listen to them again, pressing my ear to the door.

"I hate hanging around the cold. You don't want me to get frostbite, do you?" she says in a baby voice and I feel sick again.

"No, of course not," he says, though his voice betrays him.

"Yuck." Annie makes puking noises.

"Ow!" she squeals and I look at Annie, puzzled.

"I am so sorry, Claire," he says, but she's shrieking and calling him a dickhead.

"My *Dior* skirt," she wails. "See what your bastard friends have done?"

I look at Annie horrified as Harry appears at the kitchen door, and I jump a mile and start doing my hair in the mirror. Harry's face is blotchy and serious.

"What happened?" Annie asks.

"Nothing, I am a fucking moron," he says. Surely he doesn't agree with being spoken about like that.

He grabs the kitchen towel and goes back to Claire.

"So anyway?" I say, ignoring the noise in the bedroom.

"How did your night with Peter go?" I look out of the window to the drive that has swirling snow falling on it.

"It was incredible." She looks at me like she's glowing.

"You had sex?" I ask, pleased I was in the attic all night.

"Oh God, Em, you should have seen the size of it." I splutter my coffee everywhere. *Oh, God.*

"That's great," I croak.

"You don't mind if he stays with us, do you?" she asks.

"Wow, you are that serious?" I say, impressed.

"I'm not sure. I don't know if it's this place or because it is Christmas or maybe the fact it's my last year before I'm thirty," she says. Her cheeks redden.

"Good for you." I say.

"Do you want to see a picture of it?" she asks.

Oh fuck.

"A picture of what?" Claire steps into the doorway

"Oh, a rare Scottish animal," Annie says, and I giggle.

"Really?" Claire looks mildly interested

"Oh yes, the Dragopenis," she says with the most poker-face expression that makes me have to hold on to the door frame in case I wet myself.

"I've never heard of that," Claire stutters.

"It only comes out at night," she adds quickly.

"Is it cute?" she asks innocently, and I choke.

"Fucking adorable and huge," she adds.

"What's so funny?" Harry appears and we laugh even more.

"Have you heard of it, babe?" she asks Harry.

"What?" He looks confused.

"The Dragopenis?" she repeats, and my legs wobble.

"The what?" He looks astonished.

"It's a rare Scottish animal." She's confused by our laughing.

After repeating it a couple more times, Harry clicks on and takes poor "baby" Claire away before she's exposed to any 'Dragopenis'. She's probably never seen one in her life.

"So, do you want to see it?" she asks again, and curiosity gets the better of me.

"Go on then." I look and immediately regret it. We both burst into fits of giggles.

"See, you do have an idea for your art gallery!" I

say after we have calmed down.

Have I given her the idea? Am I going to find Peter with a blanket wrapped around while Annie paints him?

"Have you seen the people I work with? They'd probably have a stroke if I painted a naked man." She imitates the posh voices.

We've been to Annie's galleries before and they are full of people with tweed waistcoats. "I might have an idea, though." Her eyes light up at the thought of it.

"Is Peter still here?" I ask. He hasn't come down for breakfast.

"Of course not," she says in a dignified manner.

I laugh at her expression. She sounds disgusted. "I'm going to meet him," she adds.

❖ ❖ ❖

After getting dressed, I headed up to the attic with a cup of coffee. I turn the light on and it works.

I take a book and sit down in a chair by the window. I know where I want to go today.

The myth's history is something I want to read. I think it's so fascinating. I read the story again, overcome with emotion at the fairy having to leave her husband and child. Was he a fairy? Was he just a normal boy? The fairy flag is in a castle that's close to here, and that's just where I'm going to go.

CHAPTER 16

The rain taps against the window and sprays come through the tiny crack in the windowsill. The trees sway in the wintry breeze. If I'm going to the castle, I have to go now. I've never been surer about anything.

Excitement runs through me as I imagine what it would be like to live there. I'm going on my own with just a roadmap I found in a drawer in the kitchen. This is going to be fun.

I walk downstairs and notice Annie isn't around. Claire and Harry are sitting in the kitchen with Rog.

"Hi," Harry says. Claire has calmed down now.

I smile back, too engrossed in what I'm doing and trying to get my gloves on.

"What are your plans today?" he asks.

"I'm visiting the castle."

For a brief second, a smile forms on his face. Should I invite him to come? I don't fancy a day out with Barbie, though.

"Oh, that dusty old thing." Claire scoffs. I roll my eyes.

"It isn't just a dusty old thing, it's history," I say.

"Actually, it sounds cool." Harry stops when he sees her face.

"Well, we are going gift shopping," she announces.

Of course they are.

"Great," I say.

◆ ◆ ◆

I take my map out and head out of the door, shouting for Rog to follow me. I bundle my coat around me. It's so cold.

I am weirdly smug that Harry wants to come with me- but Claire doesn't want to see a 'dusty old castle.'

My car is parked at the end of the long drive and as soon as I get inside, I turn the heating on.

I take out my road map, ready to spread it out in front of me, and notice a piece missing. An enormous gap right beside the castle has gone. I don't remember it being like this when I found it yesterday.

I shake my head and start the car that Connie and Fergus let me borrow. They rush up the drive towards me.

"Emilia, darling?" Connie taps on the window, making me jump. I don't know what's wrong with me today. I wind down the window.

"Don't miss our carolling tonight." She winks at me and follows her husband inside the cabin. Harry's walking out of the door without Claire. He spots me and comes over.

"Yes?" I say, annoyed.

"Nothing, just take care," he says with a small smile on his face.

"You know you can join me if you like," I offer.

"I have to do my Christmas shopping," he says with a shrug.

Translation: Claire is dragging him around the shops.

"Oh well. Next time," I say and wind the window up.

Claire comes out of the cabin.

"Can you give us a lift to Portree?" he asks and before I can answer, he has already opened the doors. The cold air bursts in, making me shudder.

"Sure, just call me the taxi driver," I mumble. Harry sits next to Claire and I start the car, muttering explicitly.

◆ ◆ ◆

The car journey is excruciatingly painful. As I pass trees and fields full of animals, one of which Harry kissed on the way up here, my mind travels to the past. I bet the fairies never had to deal with annoying passengers in the back seat smooching loudly while the driver tries to navigate the road map because the map is half holes.

"So Em, urm, are you coming carolling later?" Harry tries to make polite conversation. I've already said I'm going and I'm not backing out now.

"Yes," I say to the mirror.

"Great, we'll see you later." Harry opens the door, letting in the cold. Rog barks at them. I have to hold Rog back from jumping out.

In my mind, I'm willing with all my might for Harry to get in the car and we could be like George and her cousins exploring a castle together, but he wanders across the road towards the village and I pull out, heading back onto the countryside road.

The rain is still pelting the window and the clouds don't look friendly at all.

Oh, and I'm lost. I've reached the hole in the map and have no idea where I am.

I let Rog out for a wee and now I'm slightly damp as well. This isn't how I planned today to be at all.

I carry on following the road to what looks like civilisation. *Thank god!*

My phone starts ringing.

"Hello?" I say into the loudspeaker. I stop the car. The sound on the phone is crackling. *Great.*

"Em? Hello." Harry is on the phone. Rog looks out of the window for him.

"Harry? Can you hear me?" I wind down the window and move the phone around the car in the rain.

"Em?" The sound gets clearer. "Have you arrived?"

"No, I am lost-," it cuts out.

I'm stuck in the middle of fuck knows where. This is the start of a horror film. I'm just waiting for some weirdo to knock at the window.

A tap on the glass almost gives me a heart attack. Thank god it looks like it's Peter.

"Are you okay?" the strong Scottish accent asks.

He's now wearing heavy waterproofs and green wellies. Annie's in the car parked to the side of me. Rog wags his tail, whining at them.

"I'm lost," I say.

"Get in my car. I'll tow yours home later." He nods towards his car.

I've never been more grateful to see anyone in my life. I want to throw my arms around him, but I don't think that's appropriate. Instead, I get into his truck next to Annie with Rog shaking his wet fur everywhere.

"Em, you're a walking disaster. Half of the village is looking for you," she says and shakes her head.

"Why?" I ask, feeling guilty.

"My mam said you were coming to see her and when you hadn't arrived she was worried," Peter answers, starting the car and turning on the heating.

"Thank you," I say and sigh with relief as the car fills up with warm air.

"Not a problem." Annie ruffles my damp hair. I wonder how far into their relationship they are.

"So, why are you so far out here?" I ask as we pass more countryside and the rain makes Rog bark.

"We got lost in the wild, too. Hey. Maybe we can recreate *Blair Witch Project?*" she jokes.

Peter chuckles next to her.

"Peter works at the castle. We're heading there. If you'd told us you were going, we would have taken you." She tuts.

"Someone made a hole in my map." I show them.

"Maybe the fairies are playing games with you," Annie jokes.

"That's strange," Peter mutters, making me feel nervous. Could Annie be right?

Moments later, we pull up to a huge stone pathway. The castle ahead looks absolutely massive. My heart thumps as I look around.

Again, I'm breathless. I have fallen in love with it without even seeing it inside.

"Good job it's winter. You won't catch any flies with your mouth open." Annie nudges me, and we all walk up to the door.

◆ ◆ ◆

"Emilia darling." Glenda appears at the door with her arms open wide. She is dressed in one of her power suits, with her blonde hair clipped back into a tortoise clip.

"Hi." I breathe in the cold air, suddenly feeling the chill. I'm exhausted from the journey here.

"Oh, look at you, ducky, you'll catch your death." She leads me through the doors and down the stone steps leading to a little stone café.

"Sit down, lovey," she says, disappearing behind the counter. Rog lies down next to the fire crackling against the back wall of the café. I take off my damp coat and settle into my seat.

"I can't say I'm not disappointed your man isn't here." Glenda scowls.

"Yeah, it's a shame," I say.

"I bet I can get him here," she says, and winks.

"I doubt it," Annie says. I watch her and she shrugs.

"Just tell her," Peter urges.

"Well, they were shopping," Annie says "for rings." She bites her lip.

My body shivers and I don't know if I'm cold from the rain or if I've gone into shock. They've barely been together for five minutes. I pretend not to care as everyone watches me.

I shake my head as nonchalantly as possible and sip my tea.

"That can't be right." Glenda scowls.

"We saw them," Annie says.

First, they're moving away and now they're getting engaged. I feel muddled up, like the rug of our friendship has been pulled from under me and I'm left to work out my feelings while it seems he has life all sorted out.

"You can be pissed off, you know," Annie whispers to me.

"I'm not," I say and shrug, unsure of how long I can last before I erupt in either tears or anger.

"Why are your hands shaking?" She takes my hand.

I look down at them, concentrating on the veins that look like the roads on my roadmap. I focus until they blur, then sniff back the tears. This is stupid, absolutely stupid. Of course, he would get engaged one day. But I thought it would be to me.

"Em, you silly bitch." Annie hugs me and I silently sob on her.

"All sorted." Glenda comes back with a glint in her eye. What is she up to?

"Sorry, Emilia," Peter shrugs, looking uncomfortable.

"Can I look around now?" I wipe my nose with the tissue Glenda gives me.

I leave everyone at the table and make an excuse that I want to be on my own. Well, with Rog. I don't want to show how unhappy I am with the news Annie has told me.

I run up the steps *Rocky*-style and along the castle. I don't know where exactly I am, but I find my way into another room whilst Rog sniffs around.

The booklet in the middle of the room says this is a master bedroom. The four-poster bed looks very grand, with expensive-looking furniture dotted all around.

From the window, beyond the window, the castle gardens sprawl below. Rows of spindly bushes dotted with raindrops line the paths. Even in its bleak winter state, it looks tidy. It'll be a riot of colour come spring. I could get lost in this place and not have to see a single soul again.

I watch in surprise as Harry gets out of his car, all red-faced. My heart flips, and I tell myself to behave. I can't have this all the time, for God's sake. I need to let him go. Maybe that's what I should concentrate on doing while I'm here.

I walk back through the corridor and down the steps with Rog running off, barking. Oh, for God's sake.

"Rog," I yell as he runs down the spiral staircase into Glenda's cafe.

CHAPTER 17

"Ah, there you are." Glenda's upbeat enthusiasm makes me feel uneasy.

"Glenda, what is the emergency?" Harry pants. Glenda quickly shoos Annie and Peter out.

"Oh um, false alarm," she says with a half laugh. Has Glenda brought Harry here to talk to me?

"Why don't you have a glass of fizz while you're here and then I'll give you a tour?" Glenda puts down two glasses on the table and swiftly shuts the doors. The lock clicks from the other side.

She's locked us in.

"This is fucking mental." Harry runs his hand through his hair.

"I know; we could die in here," I mock him. I have a feeling she knows exactly what she's doing. Surely, she won't let us die in here.

Harry sits down at the table staring at the door.

I desperately want to ask about the ring, but it isn't my business.

"Did you have a good shopping trip?" I start.

"Yes." He's clearly in no mood to talk.

"Harry, I know… I know you went shopping for

engagement rings." My voice wobbles, but I try not to show any emotion on my face.

"I was going to tell you eventually," he says with a shrug. Rog sniffs around Harry's feet. "What's up with him?" Harry reaches down to stroke Rog, who is now growling at Harry's shoe. Harry stands up and takes a step backwards.

"Did you step in something?" I come closer, seeing something stuck to his foot.

Harry lifts his shoe and removes a bit of scrunched up, dirty paper from it. It's all muddy and grassy, but I can just about make out the veiny roads.

"My map," I whisper. Harry opens it and puts it on the table.

"I have no idea how that got there." His eyes are wide with shock.

"You had my fucking map the whole time. I got lost because it was missing and you had it this whole fucking time." The tears trickle down my face as I explode.

"I didn't," he starts.

"I bet you had a right fucking laugh, the two of you. Let's get rid of Emilia. Ha ha."

I'm shaking so hard I can't believe he's done this. I had an idea Claire didn't like me, but I didn't think she would sabotage me.

Harry races across the room while I sob, and takes my hands, making me look into his greyish blue eyes.

"Em, I swear, I didn't know," he says and squeezes my hands.

My skin tingles with Harry's touch and I am sure for a split second he feels it, too.

I sniffle, not sure whether to believe him. He pulls me into his familiar arms. This probably isn't a good idea.

"I promise you, I didn't know." He looks into my eyes, making me feel nauseous.

"It's just too convenient."

"Well, lots of weird shit has been going on around here since we arrived," he points out.

"Like us ending up in bed together last night?" I say and he nods.

If it was any other time, without all the pressure, we would probably be laughing about all of this. I am definitely not happy. I feel stupid.

"I'm sorry I didn't tell you about the ring," he says.

"Why?" I ask quietly.

Harry sighs and lets go of my hands as if I've just shocked him. He looks down at the floor and I feel so confused.

I eye the glasses on the table. "Let's drink," I say. Hoping that will numb whatever this feeling is that makes my insides feel like mush.

Harry goes to check the door to see if it's locked. Of course, it is, and I'm sure Glenda's listening on the other side, too.

◆ ◆ ◆

Half a bottle of wine later and being trapped together isn't too bad. Being a little tipsy has cleared the tension between us.

"I should try the door again; it's been a couple of hours." I get up as Harry necks his drink.

Weirdly enough, the door opens.

"She must have got bored with us." Harry joins my side.

We're both too tipsy to drive back now.

❖ ❖ ❖

We walk up the steps to the main castle, Rog following closely.

"Damn it." Harry knocks on the main door, but all the lights have gone off and it looks like we're the only ones here.

"You wanted to explore the castle." Harry's face lights up, and I wonder if this is finally him talking. This is the most like himself he's been since we arrived.

He's changed from last year and I'm not sure it's for the best either. He's wearing fucking tweed and his hair is gelled and styled. He looks so uncomfortable in himself, like he can't decide who he is.

"Yes." I feel peckish now. We could pinch the cakes Glenda left in the café, but I don't fancy going back down there again.

I take out one of the little illustrations I

borrowed from the attic and show him. "This is why I wanted to come here and I don't want to hear about how stupid it is."

How dare Claire say anything bad about history?

"I would never." He shakes his head like he can't believe I would suggest such a thing.

"Why don't you stick up for me?" I ask.

"I don't want to fall out with either of you. You're my best friend and Claire, well, she's my girlfriend," he says.

The sun is setting now and the castle will soon be dark. We walk up a flight of stairs and into one of the rooms. I look at the picture again as Harry shines his torch around. We're apparently in the fairy tower.

I smile, looking around, mesmerised by the flag on the wall. It's old and a little ragged, but it's so amazing to be in the same room as it.

Harry shines his torch on the little inscription on the wall. The look on his face mirrors how I feel.

"It's incredible," he says and sighs.

He doesn't touch the picture, but takes the book and reads the page about the myths and fairies. The same story that Glenda said tries to get couples together through 'heaven or hell.' I do feel like there is something magical in this room.

"It is." I sit down on the floor under the fairy flag next to Harry. I am less tipsy now and instead I feel warm and excited, like we were meant to find this room.

Out of the window, the sky is completely dark but clear. We're relying on the light from our phones. I swear I can see a tear in his eye, but I don't say anything. Instead, I hold his hand and squeeze it to let him know I don't mind if he cries.

"Sorry," he says eventually. "For the way you found out."

"Finding out from Annie was pretty embarrassing," I say.

I'm really pleased we have the chance to talk. I don't know if he feels anything for me. It feels so natural, like it's supposed to happen.

I'm enjoying the warmth of his hands and his closeness. He's smiling at me just like he used to.

"I'm truly sorry," he says.

I shake my head. "It's okay," I say.

Nothing matters right now. I don't want to kill the vibe. I don't know if I'm imagining it, but Harry leans closer to me. I lean towards him and our lips meet.

Someone clears their throat, and we bump heads, trying to get apart.

"I wondered what had happened to you two." Glenda's at the door with her arms folded.

"We were just looking at the flag," I say and smile, walking to the steps to leave.

"I see, and it just happens to be inside your mouths," she says with a smirk, proud of herself.

CHAPTER 18

T he journey home feels different. Glenda drives us while occasionally glancing at us through the mirror.

Harry stares out of the window on his side, but it doesn't feel awkward between us. Rog is curled up next to us on the back seat, fast asleep.

As she parks the car, light flurries of snow whirl around us. Harry smiles at me as we all get out.

"Bloody hell, you two." Annie's voice comes from a car over from ours.

"What?" I ask innocently.

Annie hands us both of our coats.

"So?" she whispers as Harry chats to Glenda. She links her arm through mine.

"We did nothing," I say and roll my eyes playfully.

"Sure you didn't, and I'm Picasso," she teases.

We reach the Inn Keeper, where Tammy and Razor are sitting at a table with Connie and Fergus. Glenda gives us lyric booklets full of carols. Nancy agrees to watch Rog whilst we go carolling. I don't think he has it in him to trek around the cold and dark streets.

"Hey, there she is." Tammy hugs me when I sit down. "I almost thought you wouldn't make it."

If I'm honest, if the carolling wasn't today, I would have happily stayed in the castle. It was cold, but I didn't care. I felt a sense of belonging I've been missing from my life.

I've never really fit in at my parent's sweetshop. It isn't my dream job. I've been drifting through life, not sure where I'm going, but this castle made me feel at home.

"So, where is bitchfest?" Annie asks before I can. I was thinking about it, but I didn't want to ask.

"At the bar," Razor whispers.

"Honestly, this afternoon she has been complaining about everything. We left three hours early to get rid of her," Tammy says.

Sure enough, Claire is sitting on a barstool at the bar with her back to us.

Harry is still talking to the locals and I wonder if he and Claire had more of a falling out this morning than it looked. Why is he shopping for rings if he's avoiding her? Not that it's my business.

"So, lovey, I'm setting up groups now. Do you and Harry want to be in a group with your friends?" Glenda asks.

She wraps a beautiful scarf around my neck. "The fairies would want you to have it." She winks and then leaves.

"Right, shall we get this utter embarrassment done?" Annie necks another drink and when Peter joins her, he takes her hand.

"Sure." I finish my drink and zip my coat up.

"Claire, love, would you like to come with us?" Glenda asks her.

"No, thank you." Claire links her arm with Harry as I exchange looks with Annie. Of course, she's coming with us.

❖ ❖ ❖

I don't fancy trekking around the village singing, but after the first house, it's not too bad. Could I call it having fun? Maybe not that far.

We stop outside a row of houses by the port. All the doors open at the same time, and we start singing *We Three Kings* and swaying.

Annie and Peter are the loudest and the drunkest out of the group, but I admit, it's either the alcohol inside me or the looks on the villager's faces that's making me feel warm and fuzzy.

"I want to go home," Claire moans after the fourth house.

Snowflakes whirl around and, with the rain from this morning; the pavements are slushy to walk on.

"Go home then." Annie turns to her as we stand outside of the church.

"I didn't want to fucking do this in the first place." She sulks like a toddler. Harry looks uncomfortable.

"Bloody hell, Haz, just take her home," Razor says after Harry starts to go after her.

We're sick of the whinging. We're also cold but, unlike Claire, the rest of us are having a great time.

"Babe, I've been drinking," Harry says.

She's definitely not used to being told no.

"My daddy can take me back to the cabin," Claire says, getting her phone out.

"How?" I turn to Harry, who's blushing.

"Claire's dad is staying for the weekend," he mutters.

Annie pretends to retch.

"Guys, can we do this later? We are carolling, remember, be happy," Tammy hisses as she starts singing 'O Little Town of Bethlehem'. We all join in, except for Claire, who's escaped around the side of the house with her phone.

Curiosity gets the better of me and I slip away from the other side of the building to listen.

"Yes, daddy, I'm cold," she whines. I roll my eyes.

"No, no, he doesn't. I know. I think we are getting close to it. I showed him the ring I want. He said he'll show you later."

"You know it's wrong to eavesdrop," Harry whispers, making me jump a mile. He puts his hand over my mouth.

"What are you doing here, then?" I hiss, and he leans against the coldness of the house.

"Looking for you." He looks at me, confused.

"I'm here and as your friend. I want to tell you: if you aren't sure about getting engaged, then don't do it," I whisper.

He shakes his head. "I don't want to be on my

own forever," he whispers.

"You would never be on your own," I say. My heart sinks. Is this what he thinks? He would be on his own if he didn't stick with Claire.

"Shush anyway." He bats away my concern.

"He doesn't know. Yes, of course, I will," she says.

"Know what?" I ask, and he shrugs.

"I know he'll find out soon enough. Maybe I can wait until after Christmas," she says.

I look at Harry and he looks deep in thought. What the fuck is going on?

"We'd better go back or she'll see us," I whisper.

"Can we go back to the castle?" he asks.

What is going on if Harry feels like the castle is a place of safety, where no one can ever hurt him? Whatever Claire is talking about has got to him. What can be worse than being engaged to Claire?

CHAPTER 19

I wake up weirdly warm. We went back to the castle after carolling. Harry seemed deep in thought the entire time. He lies next to me, covered by a quilt. Rog is curled up at the end of the bed again.

Strange.

We didn't return to the cabin. We definitely went back to the castle after carolling.

I sit up, taking in my surroundings. Moonlight casts an ethereal glow over the surrounding clouds in the black sky. We're in the attic again. Okay, this is weird. Did we drink more than I thought? How did we get home from the castle? I clearly remember settling down for the night at the castle.

"Harry?" I shake him awake. He sits up and looks around.

"We're in the attic?" He yawns. I nod.

"Do you remember coming home?" I ask.

He shakes his head.

"Did we definitely go back to the castle last night?" I whisper, and he nods.

I feel around for my phone.

Two texts again. Maybe everyone else

remembers what happened.

OMG Em! You just left me, man. Not cool - Annie x.
Are you okay, babe? Tam.

I'm sure I got rid of my texts yesterday, but these are showing up as new from eleven pm on December the fifth.

"It's the seventh today, right?" I ask.

"Yes." Harry checks his phone.

"My phone says the sixth."

"Mine too." I frown. If this is a joke someone's playing on us, it's not funny.

"I have to talk to Claire today," Harry says.

We both get ready to leave the attic. I'm so confused. What's going on?

I wrap my dressing gown around me and follow him down the steps.

Annie's at the bottom in her nightdress.

"Is there an attic full of money that you have found?" Annie asks sleepily.

"No." I say with a forced smile, although I feel like I'm still dreaming.

"So, no progress?" she asks. "He hasn't asked you to marry him?"

I can feel a lump in my throat and a heavy feeling in my stomach. I have to hold on to the kitchen worktop to steady myself. Harry has just followed me into the kitchen with Claire, and I catch his eye.

What the fuck is happening?

"Morning." Annie smiles at Harry and Claire, then pulls the same face behind their backs as she did yesterday.

I make Rog's breakfast with my back to everyone to hide my face.

"Good morning, Emilia, Annie," Claire says with a smile at us. Annie takes her huge bowl of Cornflakes to the table and sits down. I join them, feeling like I am in an out-of-body experience.

"Where are Tam and Razor?" I ask, trying to remember where they were yesterday.

We were at the bar. I came home early, and that's all.

Annie pours herself a bowl of cornflakes.

"They slept over at Razor's parents," she says.

Harry meets my eye again.

"We were going to join their party, weren't we, baby?" Claire says and smiles at Harry.

"Yeah." Harry says while playing with his hands.

His hands are shaking. I wonder when he noticed everything was a little strange.

No one else has noticed anything different about today, except Harry. It seems no one but us is in on whatever this is.

"I'm going to the castle today," I say, mostly addressing Harry, and he nods. It's like we're communicating in code and no one else seems miffed.

"Right, all your fairies. Harry told me about that," Claire sneers. I look at him. He stares at me with his mouth open wide.

"Well, I think it's all romantic," Annie says,

starry-eyed and gooey.

I think back to yesterday morning at the table. The conversation today is the same, but no one seems to realise it.

Should I be upset that Harry could have defended me again? He doesn't look too happy at all.

"It is history, Claire," he says and shakes his head, and I shoot him a grateful smile.

Annie catches our exchange and raises her eyebrow.

"It is," I say. Claire wrinkles her nose up.

The room is silent, and my head is spinning. Has Harry proposed? How could he when he was with me?

All Annie said was that they went ring shopping. How would this play out if I went with them instead of going to the castle?

And what will happen tomorrow?

I want Harry to say that he wants to come with me this time. Maybe he doesn't know what's happening, but from the stiff look on his face, he suspects something, at least.

"Harry?" I say, and he lifts his face to mine. We just look at each other.

"Maybe he doesn't want to talk to you," Claire says venomously. My eyes meet Harry's again.

"God, we aren't going to have this all day, are we? It's flipping Christmas, guys." Annie interrupts us all.

I leave the room feeling like I am in a nightmare. What the fuck is going on? Why is today the same as yesterday?

Annie follows me into the hallway.

"So are you coming carolling tonight?" she asks. "Please Em." She bats her eyelashes at me, just the same as before. I agree before she begs again.

◆ ◆ ◆

Claire and Harry are sitting on the sofa, and I notice the obvious space between them. Am I properly awake or did we get hammered when we went to the castle and this is all an alcoholic dream?

"Isn't it a shame we can't go tonight?" Claire's voice is shrill and she ruffles Harry's hair.

"Not really," he admits.

I remember her conversation on the phone last night and wonder if that's what Harry is thinking about.

"Why not?" she asks suspiciously.

"Because I want to know what you were talking about last night," he yells.

He looks over at me and I usher Annie out of the room.

"What was that all about?" she asks.

"No idea," I say and shrug. It's not my place to tell her anything.

"I want to talk to you," she whispers accusingly.

"I know."

I freeze. How the fuck do I explain what is happening?

"Know what?" I whisper.

"I read over your shoulder what your wish was."

I'm so relieved, I want to cry. I know this is what she told me yesterday and I should remember, but a tiny part of me thought she knew what was happening to Harry and me.

"Please tell him before he moves in with Elle Woods meets Barbie," she pleads. I giggle again and she hugs me.

"I don't think I can," I say. I want nothing more than for us to be together. I am still getting mixed feelings and it isn't helping my plan in the first place to get over him. He has been following me everywhere and not her, and now he's going to get engaged.

The sound of an argument spills out from the next room before Claire stomps out of the house in tears.

"I'm going to wait for my dad to arrive." She cries and glares at me like it's my fault.

Harry comes back into the room, tears filling his eyes. What happened while I was talking to Annie? Did he confront her about last night?

"Mate, what did you do?" Annie asks.

Harry's face is screwed up, and he looks pale and tired. He doesn't go after Claire. How will this change our already strange day if he doesn't go shopping with Claire?

"I asked her something, and she flipped out." He scratches his head.

So whatever happened yesterday, Harry confronted her this morning, and she didn't know what he was talking about.

I think about the rest of the day and how it will work. Are we really doing yesterday all over again? Do I have to do everything I did? Is there a rule book to go by?

Harry stands by the door, hesitating before he leaves.

"How did your night go?" I ask Annie, vaguely, because I already know. But I have to keep up appearances.

Annie watches Harry and Claire as it started snowing again.

"It was incredible." Her face glows, and I wonder how many times we will have this conversation.

"You had sex." I state more than ask.

"Oh God, Em, you should have seen the size of it," she brags. She takes her phone out and shows me. My hands grip tightly around my cup. I can't shake the déjà vu feeling I'm experiencing.

"Great," I mumble, trying to get enthusiastic for her. I hope Harry will come back in and save me from the conversation from hell.

I watch Harry and Claire out of the window. It looks like they're mid-argument again and I don't want to bring him into the conversation, but I don't want to have the same conversation. I know what's coming.

"Is it alright if he stays with us?" Annie asks and I nod. Of course he will go back to her. The tears silently fall, and I wish them away. I just want to get as far away from here as possible. I want to go to the only place that made sense.

The castle.

"Are you okay?" Annie stops saying whatever it is she's saying and looks at me, concerned.

"Yes, of course," I say, distracted.

"I have something that'll take your mind off of Harry." She nods towards the window. "Want to see my glorious boyfriend's dick pic?" she asks, and I giggle. I can't help it.

Claire appears in the doorway and sees us giggling.

"What?" she asks and we giggle more.

"Oh, a rare Scottish animal," Annie says.

Harry walks in after her and we look at each other.

"I think we should go," Harry says, harshly. He knows what's coming.

"No, I want to see the rare animal," Claire insists.

"I don't think you do," he says, trying to pull her arm.

"Oh, Harry, it isn't going to hurt her," Annie says and rolls her eyes.

"It might bite, though," I say and giggle.

"What's it called?" Claire asks.

"The Dragopenis," Annie says with the straightest face. Even Harry can't help a smile.

"I've never heard of that," Claire says, looking between us.

"It only comes out at night," Annie answers.

"Claire, we have to go," Harry insists and leaves with poor, damaged Claire. Annie and I burst into laughter.

Annie shows me the same photo as yesterday, and that sets us off giggling. She's right, I've cheered up slightly.

"So you've got an idea for your gallery," I say. I know she won't, but it's still a fun idea.

While Annie talks about her gallery again, my mind wanders to the rest of the day. Will my clothes be in the same place as yesterday? Will Peter and Annie save me again?

CHAPTER 20

I excuse myself when Annie stops talking and go back to the attic to get dressed. I turn on the light and settle for another pair of jeans and a woolly jumper. The tears come when I pick up the fairy book and settle into my chair.

I'm not sure if I'm crying about Harry or the whole situation, but I'm thankful this room isn't well lit.

The rain outside patters against the window and I long to sit in the castle feeling cosy. But if I go too early, will Annie and Peter be there?

I head downstairs and go into the kitchen. Harry and Claire are standing in the kitchen as if their argument this morning didn't happen. Annie has thankfully let Rog out into the garden for a wee.

Harry watches my every movement and I hold my breath, opening out my map. Everything is intact, so how does it end up on Harry's shoe?

"Hi." Harry attempts to make conversation, but swallows, and gazes at me.

"I thought you were going out?" I ask, and he nods.

"I wanted to make sure you are okay. Is the map

all there?" he whispers as Claire comes over to us, looking suspicious.

"It is." I unfold it for him to look at, and then put it away.

"What's going on?" Claire asks, looking between us.

Why can't he just let her dad come and we can chat about all of this? I need to talk to someone. This is madness.

"Are you going there now?" he asks, and I try to communicate to him that if he wants to come with me, he can do it.

"Yes," I answer.

"Go where?" Claire asks.

"The castle," we both say at the same time.

Claire scoffs. "That dusty old thing."

"Don't be rude, Claire," Harry says, and he looks genuinely upset that he said it.

"We are going gift shopping," Claire says.

To look at rings. The thought appears like a bubble in my head. An annoying one I'd rather not think about.

I start doing the opening to 'Single Ladies' by Beyoncé, and Annie walks in doing the hand-turning bit of the dance.

"How do they know?" Claire asks Harry, turning to face him so quickly that I fear she might get whiplash. Harry's face is priceless. He flushes scarlet bright red.

"Urm."

I shrug. I'm not helping him out. Why should I when he's still going ring shopping with her? After our conversation last night, he still wants to marry Claire.

CHAPTER 21

I bundle myself in my coat, make sure I have everything, and mouth to Harry that he can come if he wants to, before heading outside with Rog.

I have a feeling he'll just do what she wants to.

How many times will we relive today? And why is this happening to us? Is there a reason? Or has the fact we have been here overnight upset the fairies so much they have cursed us?

❖ ❖ ❖

The cars parked in the same spot as yesterday. Did Peter bring it back? Did we drive home? How can a car magically transport itself back? I'm sure I didn't drive back here. I remember settling down with Harry.

I unroll my map to check it and notice the piece is missing again. But I checked to make sure it was fine before I left. I storm into the house, annoyed.

"Check your fucking shoe," I scream at Harry. Both he and Claire look surprised. Harry lifts his shoe and the map's there. How the fuck did that happen? I snatch it from him, feeling anger rise in my chest while Harry's eyes are wide.

"What's going on?" Claire asks, her eyes darting from me to Harry.

"I... um." Harry stumbles on his words.

"Are you two sleeping together?" she asks.

"No," we both say together.

"What is this, then?" she asks, gesturing to the map.

"It's the map," he whispers, like its magic gold dust.

I open it up, and it's the missing part. We look at each other, stunned. I think we're thinking the same thing.

"Can I come in?" Razor's Mum asks breaks through the silence.

"Yes, Mrs Brown," Harry says. She appears and smiles at us.

"I just wanted to pop in and tell you to come to the carol service in Portree tonight," she says.

Harry shuffles uncomfortably as I look at him.

"I'm not sure if I'll be back in time," I say, after explaining where I am going.

"Oh, what a shame," she frowns.

I leave them to it, unlock the car, and am greeted by Rog. At least I don't have to agree this time. I can stay at the castle instead, and I don't have to see Claire tonight. *Win, win*.

I'm about to drive off when Harry stops me. Claire is beside him.

"Can we have a lift?" He smiles, and my heart sinks and skips a beat at the same time. Before I answer, they get into the back again.

A sense of longing makes me feel uncomfortable. I need to talk to Harry about all of this, but he won't leave her side.

Why is he wasting the day doing exactly what we did yesterday when we need to discover what the fuck is going on? Is he taking any of this seriously?

"So, are you going carolling?" Harry asks.

"No," I answer firmly.

The rain pelts at the window as they get out of the car. I have to hold Rog back again.

A mean thought pops into my mind. What would happen if I went with them? Maybe I can play around with her head. Or at least ask him why he has suddenly changed his mind about her.

The thought warms me inside like I'm about to do something naughty. I should focus on the task at hand and not get distracted.

I'm sure the castle has answers to what's going on with us and, hopefully, it won't take long to figure it out and stop it. What if we miss Christmas?

I watch them disappear into the distance as I decide what to do. Maybe I can stop him from buying an engagement ring? I can tell him it's a stupid idea, not because I want him, but because it is.

Rog barks in the back and flies out of the open door before I can stop him.

What the fuck is going on?

"Rog?" I shout as I follow him. Of course, when I catch up with him, he's getting a belly fuss from Harry.

"I thought you were going to the castle?" He watches me with his gorgeous eyes.

"Rog escaped the car." I sweep my sweaty hair out of my face.

"Oh, he is a good boy. Yes, he is." Harry fusses him and he happily rolls over.

He knows what he's doing, the little shit.

"I'm sorry if I've ruined your plans," I say to Claire, who looks less than thrilled to see us.

"You haven't," she says too brightly.

Harry straightens up and takes the lead.

"Of course not." He smiles encouragingly. Does having me around make him more comfortable?

"Where to first, guys?" I ask.

I'm enjoying this, knowing Claire isn't. I'm not letting Harry buy her a ring.

"Urm well," Claire starts.

Harry freezes in place, and I ponder if Claire is repeating exactly what she did yesterday.

She walks ahead. "What's wrong?" I whisper.

"I think you know," he whispers back.

"Where does she go?" I ask, waiting for her to decide.

"Jewellers." He points to the one about four shops down with a sparkly sign.

Sure enough, Claire stops outside the jeweller's and turns to Harry. I make sure Rog's lead is tight in my hands.

"I want to go in here," she insists.

I give him a look that says *you have a choice*, but he ignores me. Claire doesn't realise we aren't following her. She's too busy leafing through necklaces.

"You know, you can say no," I whisper.

I desperately want to shake him and tell him not to do it, but that would push him away.

"Harry, baby?" Claire links arms with him and he walks off with her, but glances over his shoulder at me. I shrug and go to look around.

"You know money doesn't buy love." A voice behind me sends shivers down my spine.

I turn around and Mystic Alice is behind me in a long coat.

"What are you doing here?" I look around for Harry and Claire. They're on the other side of the shop trying on rings.

"I'm everywhere," she whispers, and without me seeing where she goes, she disappears.

A little shaken up, I find Claire trying on rings. "Where did you go?" Harry whispers.

I can't tell him everything, can I? Maybe he'd understand with all the weird shit going on.

"I got caught up in something." I don't meet his eye and he raises his eyebrow but doesn't push it.

"Can we talk more about it later?" he asks.

"At the castle," I reply.

He nods.

"I don't think you should do it," I blurt out. He doesn't look surprised. Instead, he bites his lip.

"I'm not sure either," he whispers.

His hands ball up like he's holding in the tension. Claire hasn't noticed and is trying on more rings. Harry looks from me to her and back with an expression I don't understand.

"Please don't stay with someone just because you think you'll be lonely," I whisper as softly as possible.

"I know. I just didn't think I'd be able to keep a relationship since…" he says.

"Since us," I finish off. I feel the tears in my eyes again.

"I want this one, no, this one," Claire interrupts, holding up both of her hands to Harry.

"Which do you like, Emilia?" she asks.

I get the sense she is mocking me by the smug smile on her face.

"Urn." I'm stumped and don't dare to look at Harry.

The two rings are beautiful. One has a turquoise blue stone in the middle surrounded by diamonds and the other is a plain solitaire ring with a single classy diamond.

"That one," I say eventually, pointing to the clear one. It's absolutely beautiful and I curiously think are these the same rings she found yesterday? Did I pick the right one?

Her face falls, and she makes a sort of whinging sound. "I prefer this one." She holds up the ring.

I guess I made the wrong decision.

"I was thinking of booking you an appointment with the vet to be castrated," I whisper as we walked to the car.

"Oh, ha, ha," he says and smiles, though, and it's genuine.

When he smiles around Claire, it always seems so fake. I'm surprised his mouth doesn't hurt.

"Why didn't you say something?" I hiss, feeling like an idiot.

I feel like he'll never tell her the truth, but bitch about his relationship to me.

"Why the fuck did you pick a ring?" He frowns at me. How could he possibly blame me?

Just as we leave the shopping centre, Annie arrives with Peter.

"Hey, bitches," she gives me a what-the-fuck look.

"Hi." I smile at Peter, who's doing some weird back pat with Harry. Rog jumps around everyone, whimpering.

"Well, this looks cosy," Annie says, looking at all three of us.

"I was just leaving actually," I say, using this as my excuse to get the hell out.

"Where are you two going?" I ask.

"We're going to help my mam out with the castle," Peter says and my eyes light up.

"Can I please tag along?" I beg. I'm embarrassed by how much I want to get away from these two.

"Of course. The more the merrier," he says.

CHAPTER 22

If we ever get back into the right time and place (whatever that means), will we have messed up our times by not doing everything we did yesterday? Maybe when we return, Harry will be Prince Harry or I'll be an Olympic gold medallist from Australia or something.

The car journey isn't as long as it seems and Peter easily treads over the rough terrain in his off-road carrier. I stare out of the window with my arm around Rog, thinking how weird all these events are and wondering whether when we get to the castle, Glenda will make Harry come again.

I try to remember what Glenda was wearing yesterday because it seems like everyone is wearing the same clothes and no one else but Harry and me are in on it.

"Mum will be thrilled you're here," Peter says as Glenda comes out, arms open wide, and gives Peter and Annie a huge embrace.

"Emilia, darling." She embraces me for a second time and my teeth chatter again in the cold.

"Come in, come in, or you'll catch your death,"

she says again.

We walk through the same corridors, down the same steps and into the same café as before, but this time I'm not as much in awe. The castle is still beautiful, but I'm slightly worried about what Glenda is up to. Part of me can't wait for Harry to arrive, so I can give him a damn good telling off. How dare he blame me for having no balls and refusing to say no to Claire?

Rog follows me down the little steps, sniffing around at all the unfamiliar smells and the cake aromas in the air.

"Well, I can't say I'm not disappointed your man isn't here." Glenda scowls again.

I nod, but I don't say anything. I won't burst into tears today because I'm angry, not upset.

"So what is going on with you two?" she asks.

Annie and Peter both sit down opposite me.

Annie raises her eyebrows as if interested in what I'm about to say as well.

"They all went ring shopping together like a big happy family," Annie announces.

Glenda shakes her head as if it's the worst thing that ever happened.

"Oh, how terrible." She shoots me a sympathetic look. "Well, let's get him here and sort this entire thing out."

"So, what the fuck were you doing shopping for fucking rings with them?" Annie spits disgustedly.

"Stopping him from making the biggest mistake

of his life," I hiss back.

"It is a mistake, you know," Glenda chips in, while helpfully tapping on her phone.

My stomach is heavy and I feel a little sick. Harry is probably still going to go through with it - even though he's said himself that it's a bad idea.

I won't cry this time. I make myself promise, but I can feel the tears dampening my eyes. Annie moves in closer and whispers.

"Em, you silly bitch." But instead of sobbing more, something in me snaps. I feel angry instead of sadness and desperation to get him so we can talk about it. He was weird with me on the shopping trip, and I couldn't get away quick enough – but that doesn't stop me from wanting him here now.

I glance around the stone café, and down at the cup of tea Glenda left for me. How does this amazing castle have the answers for us? It has an edge of magic to it. If we search hard enough, we'll find something to help us. I'm so sure about it.

Glenda disappears and Peter and Annie say goodbye. I'm on my own until Glenda reappears with Harry.

"You fell for it again?" I whisper.

"Guess I'm a fool," he says with a shrug. "So, Glenda, what was the emergency?"

"Oh, um, false alarm." She half laughs again and I raise my eyebrow at Harry. He knows how this works. Why has he fallen for this again? Glenda reacts like she thinks it's the funniest thing in the universe.

This time, when Glenda puts the champagne down, I don't mind that she's shut us in. It's the first time we've had to talk uninterrupted - and we get a glass of fizz too.

"This is fucking mental," Harry says, and I look at him.

"Don't start repeating yourself?" I say.

He smiles and apologies.

"So now we're alone, we can actually talk about this." I pour us both a glass of wine. We sit down on the floor.

"At least we know the door won't be locked for long," I say and smile. Harry nods.

"So, what do you think we should do?" he asks.

"Well, everyone we're with is saying the same things they said the day before, but I don't know. Let's talk about cars?" I mock.

Harry gives my shoulder a nudge and rolls his eyes.

"Was Claire exactly the same?" I ask.

"Yes. Down to putting the same earrings on. I freaked out and spilt coffee on her skirt. She stomps off in a huff.

"It's really freaky." I take a sip of wine, and the bubbles fizzle in my throat.

"Em?" he asks

"Yeah?"

"Did we fall asleep in the attic again or were we at the castle?"

"Castle." I'm sure we weren't that drunk.

"Right." He nods and downs the rest of his drink.

"What did you want to do while we're here?" he asks.

"Don't you wonder why we are in this?" I ask.

"Yes, and if I have to go ring shopping again tomorrow, I might blow my fucking head off."

"Then don't go fucking shopping," I say and roll my eyes.

"Are we allowed to do that?"

"Harry, we can do what we want."

"Well, I'm sorry. I've never had to repeat the same day. Please forgive me if I don't know how this works," he says, raising his voice to me.

"That's why I want to explore around here. I don't know why, but I feel like we might get some answers from the castle."

"Can we not just get drunk and do that tomorrow?"

"If you want," I say and shrug. "But if we repeat today, tomorrow, I want you to say no to ring shopping."

"Pinkie promise." He holds out his finger. I almost laugh at the ridiculousness of it, but then nothing surprises me now.

I hold my finger up and he wraps his around mine. Our fingers touch and I feel the static between us.

We say the ritual and then pull away.

"So, what did you find out about last night?" I ask.

He shakes his head and his hands tense into balls. I reach over and put my hand over his.

"Harry?"

He looks at me with a strange expression.

"Is it that bad?" I ask, and he reaches out for me.

"I haven't found out anything yet, but we heard her hinting at something, right? I'm not going crazy, Em, am I?"

He's inches from my face and I'm worried. I'm already getting flustered from us being so close.

"No, I was there."

"I don't want to leave this place tonight," he says eventually and I nod.

"You just want to get drunk here tonight."

He gets up, just like yesterday, or today, and checks the door. It swings open like last time.

He holds his hand out to me and I take it. It's warm and I squeeze it to reassure him. We walk up the stone steps, Rog wagging his tail, following us into the main castle.

"Where do you want to go?" I ask.

The sun is setting outside the castle windows behind the mountains, casting golden rays into the river below.

Harry must have been watching it because I don't think he's listening to me.

Rog sniffs along the floor, wagging his tail. A tourist has dropped something, and he's more than happy to have found it.

"Still want to get drunk?" I waggle my half-full champagne glass.

We're still holding hands. I could stay holding hands forever.

"Yes," he says matter-of-factly. The trouble is we still only have one bottle of wine.

❖ ❖ ❖

We walk hand- in- hand along the corridor and up the steps. On the steps is a little basket containing two bottles of wine.

With love

Glenda x

"She's sneaky, isn't she?" I say and laugh.

Harry picks up the basket, and we head into a room.

The lights flick on. French doors lead out onto a balcony with a table and chairs.

We sit down and I pour myself another drink. Rog lies down under the table.

"Do you think Glenda has anything to do with this?" he gestures.

"How could she?"

The thought has come to me, but I can't see how it's possible.

"I don't know," he says and shrugs.

"So, do you believe in the *stupid fairies* then?"

"Yes, but I'm not getting into an argument with Claire about it."

"Why do you feel you have to change for her?"

"It isn't as easy as that."

I pop the cork and start swigging out of the

bottle.

"Why do you suck up to her, Harry? I mean, look at your bloody hair and why the fuck are you wearing tweed?"

Harry sighs and stares at his glass. His hands tighten around it and he glances back at me.

"It isn't her. Her dad is my boss, and he scares me."

Of course, now it makes sense.

"So, you have to suck up to them so you don't end up alone?"

The sun has mostly gone and the night sky stretches over the river with silvery stars. It's bitterly cold.

"I thought at first it was all about the new job I've been offered but coming here has made me realise if I'm not with Claire, then how long will it be before I find someone else?"

I nod. "That's not a reason to stay with someone."

"I know," he nods.

"What will happen if you move away and then break up?" A part of me knows the answer.

"I'd lose my job; I would be on my own, far away from my friends and family." I wince a little at his matter-of-fact tone and take his hand again, squeezing it.

"You can't move away if you aren't sure, and Claire's dad can't threaten your job."

"He already did." Harry downs the rest of the alcohol silently.

"You definitely shouldn't do this."

"She wants to get married and live near her parents." His voice deflates.

"So, you have to be miserable to keep someone else happy? That isn't how it works."

He sighs and puts his drink on the table. "I don't want to, Em."

I have the craziest idea in my mind, but I don't think he'll go with it.

"Harry?" I start as confidence sparks through me.

"Mhm?" His voice was hopeful.

"If we're in this time, whatever, and tomorrow doesn't matter. Why don't you test the water? Break up with her for one day and see how you feel," I say, proud of myself.

"I think the guilt would eat me alive. And what if her dad comes over?"

"What if her dad comes over? Harry, you have an entire day. The drive here alone takes hours."

He nods whilst he considers it. "I think I will." He puts 'Last Christmas' by Wham! On his phone.

"A dance?" He folds his chair into the table to make room and takes my hand. His eyes look less troubled and I realise the weight of the world has been lifted from his shoulders. I bite my lip, hoping to be relieved of the guilt. I had an idea their relationship was bad and maybe I have been thinking he deserves it after everything that's happened.

He twirls me into his arms so our noses

touch. When this happened yesterday, Glenda interrupted us, but I'm sure Glenda won't find us this time.

He leans into me and envelops me in the most amazing kiss I've ever experienced. The kiss of freedom.

CHAPTER 23

I sit up in the attic's darkness. We definitely didn't go home last night, so the day must be the same… Again.

I can't believe Harry and I kissed last night. I can still feel the butterflies and the tingling on my skin from where we held hands and danced until we were too drunk to stand and fell asleep on the balcony under blankets.

Now, more than ever, my thoughts are on that Christmas tree. Did Harry put a message in there asking for help to get away from Claire? Maybe Glenda read it and that's why she is being so strange.

But it still doesn't explain why we are in this time loop. Nothing explains it, and I'm not sure we'll ever be able to explain it.

"Em?" Harry sits up next to me, rubbing his eyes. Rog is curled at the bottom of the bed.

"Yes?" My eyes adjust to the darkness. Harry puts the table light on.

"Are we in the attic?"

"Yes."

Harry pulls me into his arms and kisses me

again.

"Harry, you still have something to do." I resist.

"I know."

I look at my phone and it shows the sixth of December and I have the same two texts from Tammy and Annie.

OMG! Em. You just left me, man. Not cool- Annie x.
Are you okay, babe? Tam.

"Shall we go and face them?" I ask.

He squeezes my hand, and I smile. What does all this mean? What will tomorrow be like? Will he realise he wants Claire after all and I'll be hurt again?

We climb down from the attic and Annie is standing in the hallway

"Is there an attic full of money that you've found?" she asks sleepily

"Bucket loads. We have been smuggling it out," Harry teases.

Annie rolls her eyes but looks at us curiously.

Harry smiles at me but leaves to find Claire. I secretly wish him luck.

"So any progress?" she asks.

I find it weird this situation has made me question everything that I feel for Harry. The day before yesterday, I would have said our relationship is well and truly done. Today, I'm not sure where I stand with him.

"I'm not sure," I whisper.

She lets out a little scream.

"You mean there's a chance?" she asks.

Harry walks in after Claire and she takes his hand. That's when I realise Harry has bottled it. I make Rog's breakfast, shaking my head. What a fool I am.

"Good morning, Emilia." Claire smiles and I look at Harry, who refuses to meet my eyes.

Wimp!

"So, this is fun," Annie announces from the table, eating a huge bowl of Cornflakes.

"What are everyone's plans?" I ask, making conversation.

"I'm meeting with Peter." Annie smiles.

"We're going Christmas shopping, aren't we, baby?" Claire says and smiles at Harry.

"What a surprise." I swear Harry's mouth flickers into a smile.

"Claire, can we talk?" Harry leaves with Claire, and I'm left with Annie.

"So, tell me what's going on?" Annie whispers. "By the way, I read over your shoulder what you wrote on your wish."

"It's complicated," I say and sigh.

"Bullshit, nothing is complicated," she hisses back. We are both listening to them talking in the other room. Has he actually done it?

He storms out of the bedroom and slams the front door behind him. Annie and I look at each other in shock.

Claire walks out of the room, head down,

blubbering. I would feel sorry for her if she wasn't a bitch.

We watch them out of the kitchen window. Snow swirls around the windowsill.

"Do you think he's chucked her?" Annie asks.

"I don't know," I whisper. "Let's talk about something else. How did your night with Peter go?"

"It was incredible," she says excitedly.

"You had sex?" I ask, already knowing.

"Oh God, Em, you should have seen the size of it."

Harry walks into the room and I can't help giggling.

"That's amazing." I'm happy for her. Harry sits down, looking like he hasn't slept in days.

"What's amazing?" he asks.

"Sex with Peter," Annie says, and I giggle. Harry isn't fazed by her at all.

"Right." He nods.

"Everything okay?" I ask.

I hope he'll tell me exactly what happened.

"Yes. Claire is getting picked up by her dad. He wants us to have a chat." He mimes getting his head chopped off.

"Ooh," Annie teases.

"I'm dead meat." He looks at me.

I nod. "Well, at least you aren't in a relationship you don't want to be in."

"Em?" he asks.

"What?" I bite my lip.

"Come with me."

Annie hides a splutter.

"That's going to go well." She scoffs, and I try to hide my expression because I have no choice, but I'm terrified.

CHAPTER 24

We arrive at the pub just after five pm. I texted Annie and Razor, who are in a booth on the other side of the room with Rog under the table in case her dad starts an argument, or worse.

Harry orders a drink for both of us.

"Hello." Tammy walks over and hugs both of us.

"Hi, Tam." I smile. Razor waves at us, holding a dart. Something sporty is on the TV in the background and Nancy comes over with our drinks.

"If any city boy thinks they are coming in here starting anything, I will have them out of here before you can say the Loch Ness Monster." She winks at us and Harry's shoulders sag with relief.

◆ ◆ ◆

Claire arrives with her dad not long after. He isn't anything like I expected at all with his bald patch and designer suit. Nancy scoffs at him.

"No drink for me. I'm not staying," he commands before looking at us.

Claire sits next to her dad, her eyes puffy and red. Why did she even come on this trip?

"So, Harry, my son, I hear we have a problem," he says.

"Yes sir," he says. I almost scoff.

Fuck sake.

"I resign," he says confidently, although his hands are shaking.

"That's too bad." He says. "Once this gets out, no one will employ you."

Nancy comes over. "I'm sure we can find something for him to do here," she says, and winks. Harry's face lights up.

Tammy and Razor are eating snacks at their table, pretending not to listen.

"Is my daughter not good enough for you?" he asks.

"Of course she is, sir," he stutters.

"Then what the fuck is she doing crying because you left her?" he yells and even I am intimidated.

Annie walks over and sits down at our table without acknowledging us.

"Because he found someone better," she interrupts. She loops her arm through Harry's.

Claire's dad laughs and gets face to face with Annie.

Tammy and Razor stand up, ready to help.

"Sit the fuck down, grandad," she says, pushing him, and he sits down.

"My boyfriend doesn't have to deal with this shit. He isn't a piece of fucking meat you get to slam about, so I suggest you take Barbie Princess here and leave. Even if you ring every bank in the world, Harry will easily find something else. You can't force someone to love you," she adds to Claire, who yelps like a Chihuahua.

Nancy stands by the table.

"Anyone who speaks to my friend like that isn't welcome in my pub." She stands with her hands on her hips.

Both Claire and her dad stand up and Claire strolls out, huffing. Annie unhooks her arm from Harry's and winks at him.

"Bloody tell him now, I got rid of them," she whispers.

Harry hugs her and thanks her.

"Where is Peter?" I ask.

"Giving his mum a lift home from the museum," she whispers.

Peter walks in shortly after, wrapping his arms around Annie and kissing her.

"I would say this is a celebration." Nancy opens a bottle of champagne.

We all have a glass and she turns on the disco lights.

"Is anyone against a Christmas roller disco?" she loops tinsel around our necks.

"Sounds great," we all say.

❖ ❖ ❖

Nancy gives us all roller skates and clears the

tables away to leave room for us. None of us are very good, but it's fun. Rog has found a spot by the fire to cosy next to and I almost want to join him.

We all sing along to 'Lonely this Christmas' by Mud and 'All I Want for Christmas is You' by Mariah Carey.

"To Harry." Nancy raises a toast, and we copy her. Harry goes bright red but holds his glass up.

"So, how do you feel?" I ask when we reach the table.

"Like a new person," he says and smiles at me. It reaches his beautiful eyes and I can't help but smile, too. Yes, we've had a little too much to drink and I can't help but think how we only really ever kiss properly when we are drunk.

"Great." I'm genuinely happy for him.

"I'm jobless, girlfriendless and skint for Christmas," he jokes. I laugh.

"Could be worse, though."

"I could be dead?" he asks.

I shake my head. "You could be stuck in a time loop where tomorrow you have a girlfriend and a job again."

He stiffens like he hasn't realised.

"I don't want to do this every day." He sighs.

"Why don't we try to figure out how to get out of this tomorrow?" We clink our glasses.

"Do you want to go carolling with them?"

"Why not? But for now, let's dance."

He takes my hand and leads me to the floor.

He has a look in his eye that I recognise.

"You want to do *the dance,* don't you?" I ask, and he laughs.

"Yes."

Ever since we were about eleven, we've loved *Friends.* For our dance in our year six prom, Harry and I did the Ross and Monica dance. Everyone loved it, but it's been a few years since we last did it.

"Ready?" he asks.

"Ready."

"Count us down."

I count us down and we get back into the routine pretty damn quickly. It's surprising how much I remember, especially being tipsy.

Everyone erupts in cheers as Harry catches me at the end. I'm sweating and struggling to catch my breath, but he holds on to me and I wrap my arms around his neck.

"I haven't seen you do that in years," Annie shrieks, hugging us both.

"We thought we'd entertain tonight," I say. We slide back into our seats.

"Drinks on the house." Nancy comes over. "That was fantastic."

"I can't believe we still remembered it." Harry says and laughs.

"I know," I say, trying to catch my breath.

"Don't worry about the time loop," Harry says, reassuring me. I can't help but feel a little disappointed no one will remember this tomorrow.

"Did you have fun tonight?" he asks.

"Yes," I answer immediately.

Could the Fairy Pools be responsible for this? Harry had jumped in after me. Maybe the fairies thought they were doing us a favour by pushing us closer together.

"I might have an idea," I whisper and he nods while I tell him that we should jump in the Fairy Pools again.

"Okay," he says finally. "We can do that tomorrow."

"Hello, everyone, are you ready to go carolling?" Glenda asks and we all cheer.

◆ ◆ ◆

We each take a booklet and again I'm paired with Tammy, Razor, Annie, Peter and Harry.

We reach the house where we saw Claire on the phone. Harry's hands are shaking. His phone starts ringing and he jumps a mile.

"It's Claire." He answers it. I wait with the group for him to come back.

"Is he okay?" Annie asks.

"I don't know." Though I'm sure I do, and by the look of horror on Harry's face, he's discovered what happened with Claire.

"Are you okay?" I ask. Harry hugs me tightly. "What happened?"

But he just hugs me tighter and whispers for us to leave.

CHAPTER 25

I wake up again at seven am with the moon shining through the window. We're in the attic again, but this time I'm not surprised. After we had gone carolling and Harry had a phone call, we had excused ourselves and come back here.

"Em?" Harry reaches for me in the dark

"Right here," I say and smile. Harry sits me on his lap, hugging me tightly.

"Morning." I wrap my arms around him. Anyone who didn't know us would think that we were together. Rog is snoring at the end of the bed.

I check my phone again. It's still the sixth of December.

"So we're going swimming today?" he asks.

"Yes," I say. Rog loves it there, so he'll be pleased.

"Are we inviting everyone?"

He looks nervous and I wonder if he means Claire.

"I don't know. What do you think?"

"Just us," he whispers, squeezing my hand. Every nerve in my body bursts into life.

"So, how did you feel yesterday?"

Harry didn't tell me what happened on the

phone and I'm curious, but I won't push him.

"Free. It's weird how it basically didn't happen."

We walk down the attic steps and Annie is in the hallway in her nightdress.

I look at Harry, waiting for Annie to mention the attic.

"Is there an attic full of money that you've found?" Annie asks sleepily.

"No, we had wild sex all night," Harry says, so straight-faced I can't help but giggle.

Annie's eyes go huge, almost rolling out. "No way!" She gasps.

"No." I laugh and high-five him.

Harry goes through to the kitchen and I hover by the door with Annie.

"So, he hasn't asked you to marry him?" she asks.

I shake my head.

Claire appears in the kitchen, and the air feels thick and suffocating. I distract myself by feeding Rog.

"Morning," Annie says and then pulls a face behind their back.

"Good morning, Emilia," Claire says and smiles at me.

I join Annie at the table with her big bowl of Cornflakes.

"What the fuck is going on with you two?" she mouths, and I gesture towards them.

"I can't say anything at the minute," I mouth. She rolls her eyes.

"So, what are your plans today?" Annie asks me.

"I'm going to the Fairy Pools with Rog."

"I'm going shopping with Harry," Claire interrupts, not taking her eyes off of me.

"Actually, Em, do you mind if I come too?" Harry asks.

"Free country," I say.

Annie gives me a strange look but doesn't say anything.

"Oh." Claire sounds disappointed. I'm secretly chuffed.

"I might ask Peter to show me them," Annie says.

"Isn't it just a pool of water?" Claire says.

"No, it's history." I look at Harry.

"It's interesting, Claire," he mumbles, and she does a Chihuahua yelp.

I look at Annie, who doesn't meet my eyes.

"It really isn't," Claire says, and laughs.

"Of course it is." Harry gives her a hard stare and I have to hold back the laughter.

"But it isn't, baby." She pouts.

"God, we aren't going to have this all day, are we? It's flipping Christmas, guys." Annie interrupts Claire, trying to stare me out.

"No," Harry says. And I agree.

Claire stomps off into the bedroom, and I roll my eyes.

"So are you coming carolling with us tonight?" Annie asks.

"Sure." I smile and she claps her hands.

Harry sighs and goes off to talk to Claire.

Hopefully, he's gone to discuss whatever happened yesterday.

I listen by the door and hear her whining.

"I just don't like the way she talks to me, baby. She's turning you against me."

"No, she isn't." Harry's voice sounds tired, and I pretend to stand by the door, not listening.

"Anything juicy?" Annie asks. I bat her away.

"By the way, I read over your shoulder what you wrote on your wish," she whispers.

"Please tell him before he moves in with Elle Woods meets Barbie," she begs.

I sigh because if it was that easy we would, but I want to know what's going on with Claire.

I can't hear what they're saying, but moments later the door bursts open and Claire shrieks, calling Harry a dickhead.

"What the fuck is going on?" I demand.

"This is all your fucking fault." She points at me.

"Oh, for fuck's sake, get a life," Annie says behind me

Annie leads me away. "If I was you, I wouldn't get involved." We walk back to the kitchen where Rog is lying under the table.

"I did nothing wrong," I insist.

Harry comes into the kitchen. "Let's go." He practically tears my arm out of the socket and calls for Rog.

"See you at carolling." Annie waves us off.

◆ ◆ ◆

We start up the car, making sure the heating is on and Rog is settled.

Connie taps on the car window and I wind it down.

"Emilia, darling, don't forget carolling." She smiles. "You too, Harry. He nods back politely.

"So, what's going on with you?" I ask as Harry sighs out of the window.

"You saw what happened?" He shrugs. "Let's just get to the pool and get our lives back."

"No, I have no idea what's going on."

"It's Claire. She says she's pregnant," he says and sighs, running his hands through his hair. I feel like the wind has been knocked violently out of me.

"You can't go on like this every day," I say finally.

"I know. I don't know what to do. It doesn't make sense."

"If you had sex it makes perfect sense."

"Can we stay here a minute?" he asks, changing the subject as we reach the Fairy Pools car park.

"Okay." I park up the car.

Snow floats down onto the gravel, and the rain soaks the windscreen. Harry turns off the radio.

"What's up?" I ask.

"Can we go to the village Christmas tree after we've been here?"

"If you want." I think about the note I left. I want to show him so much, but what does it matter now?

"I want to tell you what I wrote." He looks at me.

"Well, I wrote I want to go to Ibiza for Christmas."

He smiles.

"Joke, Harry," I say and giggle.

We put Rog's lead on and walk out of the car park and along the trail to the top of the pools.

The wind whips around us and it's so cold, but the view is breath-taking.

The miles of mountains and countryside are making me feel less exhausted. As snow and rain battle on and the wind blows over any exposed skin. Is jumping in this pool of water going to bring tomorrow? We let Rog off of his lead.

"Ready?" Harry asks. We hold hands at the edge of the pool.

Rog barks nearby as he walks next to us.

"If we die, we die together," Harry says. The sickness has returned to my stomach.

"Let's get this over with," I say and shiver.

We walk down to the lower rock and sit down on the side. I dangle my legs over and Rog jumps into the water.

"Three, two, one…" Harry counts us down and we jump in together. I shriek when I hit the water. It's as cold as I thought it would be. Luckily, the water is only at our waists, so it could have been worse.

"What do we do now?" My teeth are chattering.

How long will it take for us to have frostbite?

"I don't know," Harry says and then smiles. "Wish for tomorrow?"

"Okay." We do a weird chattering teeth version of 'The Sun Will Come Out Tomorrow' from *Annie*.

"Can we go now?" I ask. My hands feel numb.

◆ ◆ ◆

We both get out of the water, absolutely freezing. Rog also jumps out and starts shaking everywhere.

When we reach the car, Harry wraps blankets around all of us and turns the heating on.

"That wasn't the best idea," I say, starting the car. Harry sits next to Rog and makes sure he's okay. Rog tries to lick him. It always makes my heart melt when they are together. They both adore each other.

"No, I agree. That was silly, wasn't it, Rog? Yes, it was." He fusses Rog, who's more than happy to sit next to him.

We pull out of the car park and head straight for Portree.

I look into the foggy distance. "Do you see that?"

"The woman in the road?"

The woman wears a long black coat with her hair in ribbons.

"It's Alice," I mumble to myself.

Harry's eyes are on me as she moves in the car's way.

"You're going to hit her," he shouts.

I press down on the brakes and the car screeches to a halt. Rog is howling in the back of the car.

Alice stands in front of us now, gesturing something I can't understand.

"What is she saying?" Harry asks.

"No idea. She's making a circle with her hands," I say, squinting to see better.

She walks to the side of the road and disappears. My breathing quickens and I'm frozen in the car.

Harry gets out and opens the door next to me.

"Are you okay?"

"You saw her, right? I'm not going crazy?"

"Yes, I saw her. What's going on?"

"She keeps appearing everywhere I am."

I sound like a mad person, but the coincidence sends shivers down my back.

"Is she a resident?" he asks.

"I don't know, but she was on the TV last New Year." I don't mention the fact I rang her up drunk.

"Do you think she knows?"

He is taking this seriously, and I'm relieved.

"I don't know, but I've seen her three times now around the village. Every time I see her, I get a weird feeling."

"Let me drive us back to the cabin," Harry says, and we swap seats.

"So, do you think the pool worked?" I ask, and he shakes his head.

"No, I don't."

CHAPTER 26

"If she's important, would she be in a book?" Harry asks.

We're now sitting back in the attic, ignoring everyone downstairs. No one has bothered us, luckily. Rog is curled up on the floor next to Harry.

"So, where would she be?" I look at the covers of the books about myths and history.

"I don't know." Harry flips through the Book of Myths.

I look over his shoulder at the Fairy Pools and the Flag at the Castle.

She isn't in any of the books.

I'm so confused about it all. Who is Mystic Alice, and why is she following me around?

"Do you think that's her real name?" Harry asks.

"No idea." I shake my head. It didn't occur to me she might use a different name at work. That makes it even worse.

"How can she just not be here?" Harry says with a frown.

This is all the more confusing. I have a feeling the Fairy Pools won't have reversed our time loop and somehow Alice is involved. This really is crazy.

We search for hours before giving up. The thought of one of Hannah's frothy hot chocolates seems like a much better idea.

I get into the car with Rog and Harry and we drive the short distance to Portree.

"Hello, my two favourite people." Hannah greets us with a giant smile.

We sit down at a table by the fire and Hannah leaves to get us a 'Christmas hot chocolate with all the trimmings.' Harry happily sits on a cushion in front of the fire.

"Em?" Harry asks.

We watch the crackling fire; it's all dressed in green garland and a giant wreath hangs in the middle of it. Hannah has the Christmas radio on in the background.

"Here you go. My chocolatey hot chocolate with sprinkles." She puts them down on the table.

"Thank you," we both say.

"I'm serious, I want to show you what I wrote in my Christmas note," he says

"Are we allowed? You don't want to upset the fairies." I smile. He laughs and we clink our mugs.

"I think I will take that chance," he says.

"Here you are, loveys." Hannah comes back with warm pastries on a plate for us both. I'm beyond grateful. They smell incredible.

"Just a little tip." She winks. "I wouldn't read the notes if I were you. Glenda will have you."

"Glenda terrifies me," Harry whispers to me and I nod, tucking into a pain au chocolate.

"Me too, but she could be our key to Mystic Alice. She seems to know everything about everyone."

I don't doubt for a second Glenda has specific motives for locking us both in a room together.

"Exactly." Harry tucks into a croissant.

We are silently processing what Glenda is up to when just the person walks in. I look at the clock on the wall. We would be locked in the café now if we had gone to the castle and Glenda clearly came here afterwards.

"Well, well, what a surprise to see you both here," Glenda greets us.

She's like a mum of the village to everyone.

"Hi, Glenda," I say, and she eyes up Harry, looking ecstatic.

"Are you both coming to the carolling tonight?" she asks and I feel she might combust if we say no, so we nod.

"This looks very cosy." She sits down and orders a cup of tea. It's so strange she doesn't know she's locked us in the castle twice.

"We're just having hot chocolate," I explain.

"The young people would call this a date," Glenda says and raises her eyebrows.

"No," we both say sharply, and I feel a stab in my heart.

"Oh, that's a shame," she says with a frown.

"Yeah," Harry says.

My hands grip around my hot chocolate cup.

"Now, Glenda, are you playing matchmaker again?" Hannah appears with her hand on her hips, holding a tea towel.

"Who me?" She gasps. "Of course not." Her cheeks colour pink.

"Again?" Harry asks and my ears prick up too. What does she mean again?

I wonder if Glenda knows about this time loop and is responsible for it.

"Yes, again," Hannah says and tuts. "Glenda, dear, why don't you tell them what you did?" She stands in front of Glenda, who has gone tomato shades of red.

"I ripped up your map," she mutters.

"A bit louder for the people in the back," Hannah prompts.

"I ripped up your map." Glenda looks at us and I realise she means the day I went to the castle, so Peter had to bring me to her.

"You tricked us both?" Harry asks.

"I just thought if you went together, you would have fun. You have so much chemistry. I was trying to help."

"You were interfering," Hannah says.

"I just want to know why you aren't together." She looks at us. Now it's our turn to blush, but the only trouble is, neither of us says anything. And Glenda looks like the cat that got the cream.

❖ ❖ ❖

Leaving the café, we walk silently through the village. Rog sniffs around on his lead. The sounds from the Inn Keeper suggest everyone is in there. Probably roller discoing around.

"Where are we going?" I ask.

I have my coat done up to my chin with my woolly hat, scarf, and gloves. The snow has slowed down, and the rain is a little more than a drizzle. Despite the winter clothes, I'm still cold.

"Here." Harry stops in the square in the centre of the village.

The giant tree towers into the dark clouds and the fairy lights cast beams through the raindrops.

The tree looks incredible with the notes hanging from it, delicately protected by waterproof jackets, holding the villager's hopes and dreams. I don't want to touch any in case I ruin someone's notes.

"Harry we shouldn't," I whisper.

I feel nervous about being caught.

"I know," he says, and I look up at his face.

"Harry, just tell me- you aren't terminally ill, are you?" I ask. The nerves are getting the better of me and I feel sick to my stomach.

"No, I'm not," he says.

He steps around me, holding his note in his hand like he isn't sure about this any more.

"Does Claire know what's in it?" I ask. He shakes his head.

"Forget about Claire," he says.

"Harry, if this is about Glenda…"

He puts his finger on my lips, stunning me, and steps backwards.

"Just shut up, woman, bloody hell," he says with a smirk.

He takes out the tiny note he wrote that's now getting wet, but shelters it with his hands.

"I'm sorry I haven't been the best friend to you, and I'm even sorrier for how we broke up last year."

My heart is beating so fast that I'm worried it will burst out of my chest.

"You don't have to do this."

He takes my gloved hand.

"I do. Every day I regret it, and I've never made it up to you. I now have infinite time to make it up to you."

I listen; holding my breath because I don't know what's going to happen or if anyone might come around the corner and interrupt us. This conversation, despite being almost a year too late, is finally here.

"I was fucking gutted," I admit, finally letting my breath out.

"I'm so sorry," he says and shakes his head.

I feel the tears in my eyes and thank the sky it's raining and so he probably won't notice.

"So, what's this all about?" I ask.

Harry turns the note to me.

Em, I'm so sorry. I love you still.

I involuntarily gasp. He tries to take the note back. "You can tell me I'm a stupid idiot if you want to, but we should have never broken up."

I see the tears in his eyes and guess how much courage it must have taken for him to show me this.

"What about Claire?"

He shakes his head. I don't know how exactly to feel about this.

"I honestly don't know," he says. He holds me in his arms. His coat is soaked, and I'm nervous. I wish we'd had this conversation before his girlfriend discovered she was pregnant.

"Mine says the same," I whisper and feel his arms tighten around me. "I never stopped loving you."

"I'm really sorry," he says again against my hair. "I'll make it up to you every day, even if we have to the same day over and over again."

What is going to happen every day? Now we have this out of the way. Will he still go back to Claire? Will Claire just keep telling him about the baby over and over again? Are we going to try again even if we can't make it work?

"I don't want it to go wrong again." I start crying and feeling like an idiot.

"That's why I'm so afraid to be in a relationship."

He wipes my eyes. I am already exhausted by this time loop. How many more times do we have to repeat today?

"What do we do about Claire and your situation?" I ask.

Harry shakes his head while I'm in his arms. "I have no fucking idea," he whispers.

"Can we go back to the lodge?" I ask.

The rain has soaked through my coat and I'm icy cold. I see the crowds carolling together and huddled in the cold, and I'm glad we skipped out on it. All I want to do is cuddle this man and never let him go again.

CHAPTER 27

This time, when I wake up at 7 am, I'm not surprised we are in the attic. We had changed our clothes and then had gone straight up to the attic after our envelope confessions. So sitting up and seeing the moon out of the window is comforting. I'm basking in the hope that today will be the seventh of December and we'll have broken the loop.

It's so dark for the time of the morning, and I snuggle back into my blanket. Why do I have to get up just because I'm awake? If yesterday didn't break the loop, then what would? Would we ever age? Would Harry have to constantly break up with Claire?

It's probably best not to think about that and hope somehow we figure this out.

I look at my phone. Two texts were flashing again. Harry sits up looking around.

"Em?" he says into the darkness.

"Here," I say. I feel for Rog at the end of the bed.

"Morning," he says, and blindly reaches for me. I shuffle closer to him.

"So it didn't work?" he asks

"I don't think so."

I check the date on my phone the sixth of December again.

"So what're today's plans?" he asks. I am sitting so close to him that our legs are brushing together.

"I feel like we have done everything, but nothing is working," I say.

"There has to be something," he says.

"You need to go downstairs," I remind him. He groans and I get that he doesn't want to, but he brought Claire here. She's his responsibility.

Annie is standing in the kitchen in her nightdress again when we come downstairs.

"Is there an attic full of money that you have found?" Annie asks sleepily.

"Not exactly," Harry says.

He sits down and pulls me onto his lap. Annie raises her eyebrows.

"What's going on with you two?" She hands us a cup of coffee each.

"We aren't sure yet," I say

"We are going day by day," Harry replies.

"That is great guys, but tell-" She cocks her head to Harry and Claire's bedroom door and I get off of Harry's lap. Minutes later, Claire walks in.

"Good morning Emilia." Claire says and smiles. I smile back. I can't wait to never see her again.

The table is tense as Harry hands Claire a drink and then she sits down next to Harry. I make Rog's breakfast for him.

"So, what is everyone doing today?" Annie asks.

"We are going shopping, aren't we, babe?" Claire asks.

"Actually, I was hoping Annie and Emilia will come with us?" Harry looks from Annie to me.

"I am meeting Peter later, but sure," she says, and I nod.

"I was thinking about going to the castle, but, okay," I answer, just as surprised.

"Of course- to see your pathetic fairies," Claire sneers.

"It's an interesting piece of history," I say.

"I think it's romantic," Annie adds.

"It is. Maybe you should read about it," Harry says to Claire, who gasps.

"Why do you always stick up for your bastard friends?" She gets up and storms off like a toddler.

"So, how was your night with Peter?" I ask, trying to not give her a chance to ask about us because I have no answer for her, and I don't know why he wants us to go with him.

We hear the argument in the bedroom between Harry and Claire.

"It was incredible." She smiles smugly. I smile at her. I am genuinely happy for her.

"Your bastard friends are always ruining everything. Can't you see they are turning us against each other?" I hear Claire shout.

"Did you?" I ask, slightly louder to drown out the arguing. We move back into the kitchen. I don't care what Claire thinks of me, and I'm sure Annie doesn't either.

"Oh God, Em, you should've seen the size of it." Her eyes are enormous and she is smiling at me. I splutter out the coffee again even though I've heard it enough times now.

"That's great." I choke.

"You don't mind if he stays with us, do you?" she asks innocently, and I shake my head. She looks so happy.

"Do you want to see a picture of it?" she asks and I shake my head. I don't need to see it again and if I told her, she would think I'm weird. How do I know?

"A picture of what?" Claire sits down opposite Annie, sulking. Harry slams the bathroom door.

"Oh, a rare Scottish animal." Annie starts.

Oh God, not this again.

I use that as my cue to leave and head into Annie's bedroom. I haven't been in here much.

"Hey." Harry is standing against his doorway, and his hair is wet.

"Hi," I say. "Is everything okay?"

He comes in and sits on the bed and I realise he is only wearing a towel.

"I don't know." He shakes his head. "Do you really think I've changed that much?"

"Yes. How can you not see what she is doing to you?" I ask, softly.

He takes one of my hands.

"I am beginning to, but I don't know what to do about it," he says.

"I don't know. We need to get out of this loop first," I say.

We hear Claire from the other room shrieking. Annie has shown her the Dragopenis, and she's probably freaked out.

"I'm so confused about everything," he says.

"Why?" I ask.

Harry kicks the door shut. Rog looks up but lazily lies back on the bed.

"I'm no biology teacher, but she can't be pregnant. The last time we slept together was… Well, quite a while ago," he whispers.

"And you haven't since then?" I quiz him.

"Of course we did before, but the relationship is new. Even you know I wouldn't have sex with someone new without using something."

"So you think she is trying to trap you?"

"Yes, and I think her dad is all for it."

"Then why the fuck are you dragging us ring shopping?" I hiss.

He's making us all have a miserable day. I don't particularly want to spend the day with Claire.

"I'm going to get it out of her and I need your help," he says. He looks determined, and I can see the bags under his eyes. I didn't notice them before.

"You are an idiot," I say and shake my head and stand up. He spins me so our noses are touching.

"I know."

My head is spinning and I think back to the

days when we just slept together for fun and our feelings meant nothing. Now, though, we've let them take over us as friends or whatever we are at the minute.

"I'm so confused." I admit. I don't like not knowing where I stand and if I'm being played or not. How can we start something new on these grounds?

"I know. I'm sorry," he says and strokes my head and I feel his stubble against me as he kisses me.

"I just want to know where I stand."

CHAPTER 28

Annie comes barging into the room and we can't excuse what we're doing. And then I think about it. I'm not doing anything wrong. I'm not the one in a relationship.

"What the fuck?" she screams and then clamps her hand over her mouth.

"Your fucking girlfriend is in the living room having a meltdown after seeing Peter's fucking ding-a-ling and you two are… Whatever you are doing," she hisses.

I can't help but giggle at that. Claire is too prudish to not be disgusted by Peter's 'ding-a-ling.'

"What is going on?" she asks, her arms folded like she is our parent telling us off.

I look at Harry, who really needs to say something. Have I been the fool all along? I feel a wave of nausea.

"She isn't my… " He says and squeezes my hand reassuringly.

"Which one? Because from here it looks like you have two," Annie says sarcastically.

Harry cups my chin, making me look at him. "Em," he says, and I feel the tears falling. Is this confirmed? What is going to happen now?

"Can you tell Barbie to get the fuck out of here, then?" Annie asks.

"Actually, Annie, can you help us with something first?" Harry asks.

❖ ❖ ❖

Annie has always enjoyed being in on everyone's gossip. She hates people whispering to each other.

We leave the house after Connie and Fergus' quick visit. Claire is in the back with Annie slowly becoming her new 'bestie.'

I'm holding Harry's hand and getting butterflies in my stomach.

"I can't wait until your wedding," Annie says enthusiastically

"I know, my daddy is paying for it and has told me to pick whatever ring I want," she says smugly to Annie.

I roll my eyes at Annie's acting, but Claire is lapping it up.

"OMG, I love ring shopping." Annie says and claps. Minutes later, we arrive at the shopping centre. The same one as the other day.

"Me too guys." I join in. Annie is taking the role of bestie a bit too far.

Even Harry raises his eyebrow.

"I am sorry for what I said about you," Claire says, and I just nod.

We let go of each other's hands as we walk into the shops. I feel slightly guilty for leaving Rog at home.

"So, what are you looking for?" Annie asks, dragging Claire to the rings.

"Peter is going to think I am a right knob head looking at rings. We've only slept together once," she says. I smile at her conversation.

"You okay?" Harry whispers, making me jump.

"Yes," I say and turn around. He smiles at me and it reaches his eyes, and for a second I wonder if he has forgotten Claire is here.

"You know money doesn't buy love." Another voice behind me sends shivers down my spine. I look over and Mystic Alice is there in the same long coat.

"What are you doing here?" I ask, thankful that Harry is here.

"I'm everywhere," she says and turns away.

"Please don't leave," I yell after her, but it's too late. She has left the shop.

"She's seriously fucking creepy." Harry shakes his head. All the colour from his face has drained.

"What the fuck does she mean she's everywhere?" I ask, looking around. She definitely left, but that doesn't stop the paranoia I feel.

"No idea," he says and we walk over to Claire and Annie, who are both wearing rings.

"Why are you trying them on?" I ask. I feel like Annie has forgotten this is all pretend and might trade me in for Claire.

"We wanted to see how they would look," Claire says, holding her hand out.

"Which do you like best, Em?" Annie asks, dancing to 'Single Ladies' by Beyoncé in the middle of the shop.

The rings are the same as before. I look at Harry, who just shrugs. *Well, thanks for the bloody help.*

"I like the plain one," I say again, knowing that Claire prefers the blue one and not giving a damn.

"Me too," Annie says, flashing it.

Claire looks slightly disappointed, but agrees.

I'm a little confused as to why he's just paid for a ring as we walk out of the shop with it in a bag.

"What's going on?" I ask Harry.

"I'm hungry," Claire whines.

"Okay, let's get lunch," Harry says, opening the door to a small café.

"Hey good looking." Peter whistles to Annie and she spins around to face him. They start disgustingly snogging each other's faces off.

"Hi, Peter." I wave, and he just puts his hand up, still attached to Annie.

"I will order our food, shall I?" Claire takes Harry's card and goes to the counter.

"So, how are you going to get Claire to admit to lying?" I ask.

Harry nudges me and takes out a pregnancy test that looks like it has been coloured in.

"Wow." I gasp, astonished at the lengths she would go to.

"Annie found it in the bathroom after talking to Claire when we were in the bedroom," he says.

"Why the fuck did you buy her a ring, then?" I ask.

"I'm keeping up appearances," he whispers, and Claire comes back with drinks. Peter and Annie come back to us. "So guys, if you don't mind, we are going to visit Peter's mum," Annie says.

We say our goodbyes and sit down.

I'm on my own with them both. Great. I wish I could be at the castle or anywhere else.

"So this is nice. We've finally bonded!" Claire says, stroking Harry's hair.

"Babe, why didn't you put the gel in today? You know I like your hair styled."

"I like my hair normal." He shrugs.

He's finally wearing one of his 'Harry' jumpers. A deep red one with a slogan on it, and it's better than the tweed shit.

"Well, I don't." She slumps in her chair.

Harry stays quiet and I kick him under the table. Let's get this shit over with. Claire continues.

"So Emilia, will you be coming to our spring wedding?" Claire asks.

"We need time to settle into our home, and of course, I will be…" She stops herself and blushes deeply.

"Huh?" Harry asks, like he hasn't been listening.

"Will be what?" I ask, feeling like she might have slipped up.

"Oh, nothing." She shakes her head going

beetroot.

"Will be what Claire?" Harry asks so sternly she winces at his tone.

"Showing," she whispers and takes out a test in her pocket.

I look at Harry, who hasn't reacted. This is his big moment. What the fuck is he waiting for?

"You're pregnant?" I ask and look from Claire to Harry.

"Are you?" Harry asks, and takes the faked test from her. The lines go over the white of the test.

"Of course, babe," she says with a giggle. She puts her hand over Harry's but he pulls it away.

"Have you fucking told anyone?" Harry asks.

Claire winces again at his language. Harry is standing over her looking intimidating and I have to tap his arm that he is going a little too far.

"Only my dad," she whimpers.

"How long ago did you tell your dad?" he asks.

"The day before we went carolling." Tears fill her eyes.

"You are fucking unbelievable. This is why I have your dads blessing to marry you. Is this why he has given me a better job?" He yells.

"Harry?" I start.

"No, she has put all of this pressure on me to propose and move away from my friends and family. The lines don't even fucking look real." He throws the test at her and she yelps. Harry grabs my hand and we leave.

Fuck.

CHAPTER 29

"At least you know the truth now before you married her," I reassure him.

We made a detour to pick up Rog and now we're at the castle. Glenda is nowhere to be seen.

We've found a room down some little wooden stairs that lead to a very old-fashioned kitchen. Rog is off of his lead and trotting around, sniffing out the pantry.

"Her dad thinks she's pregnant, and she's lying to both of us," he says. He sits on a little ledge in front of the window. There's a clothesline with a lever to turn it in the corner of the kitchen. The entire place feels magical, and not the kind of place for this discussion.

"Surely that makes it easier to break up with her," I say, stroking his hair. He holds my arm close like he's hugging me.

"It does."

"I'm really sorry."

"It isn't your fault." He pats for me to sit down with him. I perch on his lap and he turns me to kiss him.

I wrap my arms around him. This is how I want to be.

"Em, you've always been here for me and I've taken you for granted," he says and nuzzles into my neck.

"Don't be stupid,"

He looks up at me seriously. "We need to get out of this mess,"

"How though?"

"Do you think Glenda knows?" he asks, and I'm silently thinking. How would she know? She hasn't shown any inclination that she knows.

"No," I say finally.

"Really?" he asks. His arms are still around me.

"How can she?"

It's a little cold now and we're still sitting on the old tiled floor. We probably shouldn't be here.

I love the castle's towering past and the thought that at one point it was full of people who had no idea they would be a part of its history.

"I don't know, but she has been playing cupid. It's like she's obsessed and I just don't get it," he says.

"I know it's weird that she's determined that we should be together,"

"What do you want to do?" he asks.

"Now?" I ask.

The sun has gone mostly down and the kitchen is shadowy.

"No." He turns to me, looking serious. "Us."

"I don't know." I turn to him. "How can we have a

relationship when you have to break up with your girlfriend every day?"

He kisses me to show that he loves me.

"Look, I know it's not ideal and if we could, I would leave this loop right now. But we're in this for god knows how long. When we get out, I want us to be together," he says.

"So do I, but what if we never get out?"

A feeling creeps over me, making me shiver. What if we never get out? I start to feel claustrophobic, like I'm unwillingly trapped.

"If we never get out, we can live out here. It doesn't seem like anyone comes here."

He's trying to be funny. I look around at the kitchen. We can't hide here forever.

"What about your job and our lives? What about our parents?" I ask.

"I don't know, okay? I can't answer any of your questions. If, and that is a big if, we don't get out, then we'll figure this out." He takes my hands to stop me from shaking and looks at me with his beautiful eyes.

"I'm sorry," I say.

A lump rises in my throat

"It's okay, Em. If I have to break up with Claire every day, I will."

I nod.

"As for our parents, I have no idea. I also don't know about Christmas either. What I do know is we should talk to Glenda."

We stand up off of the floor and my bum is cold

and numb. "Rog," I say and snap his lead on.

◆ ◆ ◆

Glenda is in her car as if she's waiting for us.

The museum is closed now, so she hasn't come back to work.

"I wondered what had happened to you both." Glenda gets out of her car looking suspiciously at us. "You're going to be late, but thank god I found you." She purses her lips, looking at us through the mirror.

"Sorry," we mumble like schoolchildren.

"I don't mind you both being here. I'm pleased you have a fascination with one of our biggest tourist attractions," she says proudly. "We don't get as many young tourists coming here, but you two are a breath of fresh air."

We make our way through the deserted roads to the centre of Portree, where everyone has gathered around.

"Bloody hell, you two." Annie's voice comes from the car next to ours. She must have just arrived with Peter, all dolled up.

"We got lost." I stand at the side of the road waiting for Rog to do his business.

Annie eyes us up. I'm not surprised after lunch with Claire. I look around for her. Ha, she already left?

Harry and Glenda walk off chatting. Are they talking about me? It's stupid, and I'm not going to leave Annie.

"So, did anything happen?" Annie asks, and I nod. She puts her hand over her mouth.

"You know, Claire stayed at the house until we left. Trying to call Harry," she whispers.

"Where is she?" I ask. Might she appear over the mountain like a monster? No more drama tonight, please!

"Drinking," Annie whispers. After I pick up Rog's poo, we stroll into the Inn Keeper. Tammy and Razor sit at a table with Razor's parents. The back of Claire's head is visible, but where's Harry?

My phone buzzes. It's Harry.

We're outside. Come and join us.

I unhook my arm from Annie's.

"I've just had a text from Harry." I hold up my phone.

"You need to tell me what is going on with you two,"

"Hey, there she is." Tammy interrupts us with a hug, and I make my excuses to leave. Tammy and Annie agree to take Rog and he makes himself comfortable underneath the table.

Harry and Glenda are on the bench outside the Inn Keeper.

"Hello." His face brightens up when I arrive. Carollers are already filing out in their groups with no sign of Claire.

"This isn't a private conversation, is it?" I ask, and Harry blushes. What are they talking about?

"Of course not, lovey." She pats the bench next to

her and I sit.

"So what's going on?" I ask.

"I've been enquiring about a job over here." Harry fiddles with his hands.

"But the journey takes hours. You can't possibly do it," I say.

"Have you not discussed it?" Glenda frowns.

"I wanted to talk to you first," he says to Glenda, whose cheeks flush with delight. "I'm thinking about moving here, Em. I was wondering if you'd want to, as well."

I feel like my life has been pulled from underneath me. Move here and leave everything? What if we never get out of this loop?

"But what about…?" I trail off.

Has he told Glenda anything? She's really pushing for us to get together. I know she wants me to throw my arms around Harry and say *yes, of course*.

"Have you even mentioned it?" I ask.

"No," he says.

"Glenda, can we talk to you?" But what exactly do I want to say?

CHAPTER 30

"Emilia?" Glenda says.

The conversation we had was weird. We brought up the time loop. We didn't use the word, but Glenda suggested the "fairies" would do what they must to bring us together and if we were supposed to be together, we shouldn't push it away. She isn't being very helpful. But I'm almost certain she knows what's going on. Did the same thing happen to her and her husband?

We break off into our carolling groups again and Glenda calls me over.

"Yes?" I turn around. Harry also turns to face her. She drapes a scarf around my neck and whispers about the fairies again. Before winking and going off into her group.

❖ ❖ ❖

Outside the first house, we start with 'We Three Kings'. Everyone is drunk except me. We've been taking it in turns to let Rog sniff and go to the loo if he needs to.

Doing this sober is way worse than doing this drunk, and I'm not really in the mood for it.

The magic of Christmas seeps from under every door and fills the faces of the locals as we sing to them.

"You okay?" Harry whispers.

"Yes," I whisper. He squeezes my hand.

"Do you want to ditch everyone and talk about it?" he asks and I nod.

We walk up the hill towards the Inn Keeper, but Harry stops before we arrive.

"What?" I ask when he hides behind a stone wall.

"Claire's dad's here."

Of course, I think back to the night when Claire was on the phone with her dad.

Harry stands up. His hands are shaking. "I'll be two minutes," he says and opens the doors to the Inn Keeper.

"Are you fucking crazy?" I shout at him.

"Maybe." He turns around and his mouth twitches into a smile. Has all of this sent him insane?

I watch through the window. Harry approaches Claire's dad. I see him nervously messing with his hands behind his back.

I can't hear what they are saying, but minutes later, Harry comes out with a relieved smile on his face.

"What happened?" I ask.

"I quit my job," he says.

I don't want to burst and remind him he's only jobless until the morning.

It's already dark.

"Are you having a late twenties crisis?" I ask as we walk towards Annie's car.

"No. For the first time, I'm having the time of my life." He starts whistling the instrumental tune of the song.

"You hate that song," I say.

"No, I hate the film," he says and takes my hand.

"Em, I finally feel free. Free of everything," he says and inhales, letting it all out.

He kisses me on the cheek and I feel uneasy. What is going to happen tomorrow, when he still has a girlfriend, and a job, and the conversation with Glenda hasn't happened?

All three of us arrive at the cabin, and it's dark and cold. Harry puts the fire on and we cosy up on the sofa with Rog on our feet.

"What did you talk about with Glenda?" I ask, watching the fire flicker. I make hot chocolate and revel in the warmth and cosiness of the cabin.

"Moving here," he says, and I look at him.

"Are you seriously going to? What about the loop?"

"When we break out of this, I want to move here… With you."

I think of my life at home. My little flat isn't too bad. The area is fine and the neighbours aren't bad.

My job though... I've wanted to leave for ages. I don't want to announce to my mum and dad that I'm nearly thirty and I don't want to work in their sweetshop any more. Lucy and Dan both make fun of me for not being independent.

"But what will I do?" I ask. He hasn't thought it through. The cabin is a rental for the holidays, it isn't like we can move in here, and what about work?

"Glenda was talking about your love for the museum; she said she could sort something out for you. Don't you see it as a new life for us both, and Rog too? We could be happy here together." He looks hopeful and I feel a spark of excitement I've never felt before.

"I want to talk to you about Glenda," he says.

"What?" I bite my lip.

"Something she said just makes me think she knows." He takes a sip of hot chocolate.

"Really?" I say.

"She said whatever you're looking for is where you want it to be."

"How does that mean she knows?" I ask, stumped by the riddle. What the fuck does that mean? I groan. I was never good at riddles.

"Well, I asked that, and she said you'll know soon enough. Just keep looking,"

I yawn. Maybe Glenda knows, maybe she doesn't - but something crazy is going on. I put my half-finished hot chocolate down and cosy up to Harry. Harry picks me up and helps me into the attic, calling for Rog to follow.

"Night, Em," he says into my ear as I fall asleep.

❖ ❖ ❖

When I wake up again, the moon is glowing. I look at my phone and see the date is still the sixth of December. Nothing has changed. We will still have to go carolling and Harry still has a girlfriend and a job.

I turn my phone off, not reading the texts again.

"Em?" Harry sits up next to me, reaching his hands through the darkness until he finds me. Rog is curled at the end of the bed.

"Yes," I say, and he pulls me close to him.

"What's the date?" he asks.

"The same," I say, and he groans.

I think his bubble has burst, and he realises yesterday meant nothing. He still has Claire and his job, and yet again yesterday was pointless.

I lie against his chest as it rises and falls with his breathing. His heart beats a comforting rhythm in my ear. "I need to get away from her. I can't go shopping again, Em,"

"Don't then," I say simply.

I'm slowly learning there are no rules. We can do anything we want. We could even run away for the day. That sounds perfect.

"Let's go out for breakfast," I say.

His eyes light up and I can tell he wants to.

"Is there a lot of money in that attic or

something?" Annie yawns as we come downstairs dressed.

My stomach is rumbling and I can't wait to get to Hannah's for breakfast.

"Bags of the stuff," Harry says sarcastically.

"We are secretly rich," I add.

We walk into the kitchen and Annie hands us both a cup of coffee.

"So cut the bullshit. What is happening between you both?" she asks.

"We are giving it another go," Harry says and squeezes my hand.

"Hallefuckingllejah." She cheers.

Claire comes out of the bedroom, her arms folded, and she is giving all three of us the death stare.

"Show time," Harry says and winks before he disappears with Claire.

"So that's great news, Em," she whispers.

"It is," I say and smile.

How will I tell everyone I might not be going home? The thought of it all makes me sizzle inside. Like an adventure. I still have this niggling worry in my mind when I think about how we're going to afford to live here.

Claire comes out of the room crying and this time Harry doesn't go after her. I can tell he's relieved by the look on his face.

Annie slaps him on the back. "The man sees sense." She does a little cheer and I laugh.

"So, what are you doing today?" I ask her, even though I could quote her plan word for word.

"I am meeting Peter; he's showing me where he works."

Of course, we already know he works at the museum and I don't want to freak her out by knowing stuff I shouldn't know.

"Sounds great." I grin.

"Have you been to the museum yet?" she asks, and I have to think carefully about how to answer. I can't say yes, I've been every day with Harry - because I can't possibly have.

"Yes," I say finally. "You know I love a bit of history."

I bet the fairies never had this problem.

"You do, and I need inspiration for my painting," she says with a sigh.

"You still haven't found anything?" I ask.

The strange thing is acres of trees and mountains surround Annie. Yet she can't see the beauty in it to paint. This place is a fairy tale. It's incredible.

"No." She shakes her head.

"Can't you paint Peter?" Harry asks.

"Oh god no. Have you seen the snobs in the gallery? They would have a heart attack if they saw his thing." And we all start laughing.

"Maybe it's time to change the norms?" Harry shrugs.

Annie nods like she's about to form a speech on feminism.

"I wonder what Peter would think of it?" she says and giggles and I start giggling again. This conversation is a weird one, considering they've only slept together once.

"Shall we get going?" Harry asks.

He stretches his arm out to me, and I'm dying to ask what happened with Claire, and if we have to face her dad again.

"Come on, Rog," I call for him to follow us outside.

"So?" I start, as we get into the car and Connie and Fergus knock on the door to remind us about going carolling. Rog barks at the sudden noise.

"What?" Harry asks, getting in the passenger side.

"What bloody happened?" I ask impatiently.

"Oh, right," Harry says, and I roll my eyes. "Her dad is picking her up later."

"Wasn't he going to stay for the weekend?" I ask and bite my lip.

"Can we not do this?" he says and we're silent. We'll never get out of this if Claire is hanging around.

"Fine," I say and shut the door a little too hard before going into the café.

◆ ◆ ◆

Hannah is standing behind the counter wearing a light blue flowery apron.

"Hello, what can I get you?" She greets us

warmly, as if we've always been friends.

"A fry up please," we say together.

"You know, in the olden days, if you cracked an egg, and it didn't run, they said you'd have good luck for the year." She puts down a bowl of water and Rog laps it up.

"Do you think that's made up?" Harry whispers when she has gone.

"Probably, to scare the folks into thinking they'd have bad luck."

"We can't have worse luck than we already have," he says.

It's true. What shittier luck than spending every single day on the sixth of December? Christmas is so near, yet so far away. I feel a rush of nostalgia. I love this time of year. This village knows how to make it feel special. Right now, the Christmas music with the sound of the fire crackling brings me comfort.

"Here you are." Hannah puts two gigantic plates in front of us. "Well, would you look at that, two perfect eggs."

The eggs are heart-shaped and the yolk in the middle looks one second away from bursting.

"This looks amazing," I say, and we thank her.

"Why does it feel like everyone knows?" Harry asks.

I look at Hannah, who's now whistling 'Last Christmas' by Wham.

"It does," I agree and eat up the mushrooms and tomatoes. I already feel warmer. In spite of the draught from the door letting the rain in.

"Do you think Hannah will give us a proper answer with no riddles?" he asks.

"No idea." I shake my head.

Hannah comes over to make sure we are okay.

"Yes, thank you," we say politely.

"Hannah, why is Glenda so interested in everyone's love life?" I ask.

"Glenda believes in the whole true love thing. She met her husband through something that happened many years ago. I can't remember exactly what she called it, but she said it was like going round and round in circles."

The hair on the back of my arms stands up, and a shiver rushes through me. Round and round is exactly what Alice said. Did Glenda go through the same as us?

"Are you okay, Em?" Harry eyes me up suspiciously.

"Oh, love, you've gone pale," Hannah says worriedly.

"Yes," I squeak.

I don't know if I want to get out or press Hannah for more information.

"Well, anyway, Glenda wants to make it her mission as councillor to encourage love on the island because of all the 'myths'; it's hard not to fall in love with it."

"Did she mention exactly what happened?" I ask.

"No, she just said she knew then that he was for her. It's very romantic." She is tearing up. "I think she sees you both in her and Joe." She looks from me to Harry, who takes my hand.

"If you get her drunk enough, she might tell you," she whispers.

Would she tell us anything if she was drunk? Does Hannah know more than she's saying?

"If you can handle anything the fairies throw at you, you're truly meant to be together." Hannah says with a sparkle in her eyes.

"We've been through enough," Harry says.

"Yes, we have," I agree.

"Then maybe the myth is right, and it has taken a little more time for you both to see it yourselves," she says.

"We've been absolute idiots," Harry admits.

"We ruined our friendship when we started sleeping together casually."

"Yeah, and since then we haven't found the balance of friendship and casual. Every time we dip into couple territory, something goes wrong," he says.

"Well, maybe the fairies guided you onto the island to make you see you're supposed to be together. Do you believe in fate?" Hannah asks, her eyes sparkling.

"I don't know?" I stutter.

Fate is the crap in cheesy films and books, not real life. But then again, who am I to question anything when this island is full of fairies and myths that are truly amazing?

"Fate works in strange and mysterious ways,"

she says, and taps her nose.

I take a swig of my coffee, deep in thought about whether fate is messing with us. It isn't funny. Is fate laughing to itself? Is fate a real person? I feel like I'm answering philosophy questions here. We'll be onto heaven and hell soon.

Bloody hell.

"I am surprised you didn't say yes," Harry says after Hannah excuses herself when another customer comes in.

"To the fate thing?" I ask and he nods, taking a bite of his toast.

"Yes, and before you ask if this is fate, then I have no idea but fate definitely has a dark sense of humour," he says, and I can't help but giggle.

"The thing is, though. It's worked, hasn't it?" he says.

"Well, yes, I suppose."

I can't think about any of this. If fate is real, then what the fuck else is real?

"I'm also finding this difficult," he whispers.

"I just- I don't know," I say hopelessly.

"I was right about Glenda though," he says.

"Yes."

I think about the stupid riddle 'Round and Round'. Is that the days going round and round? Is it something to do with breaking the damn loop? Is the loop round and round?

"So are you actually okay?" he asks.

"Yes. I think I have some explaining to do," I say. I need to tell him all about Mystic Alice.

CHAPTER 31

I explain everything to Harry while we sit in front of the fire drinking our hot chocolates and stroking Rog, who is stretched out next to us. Harry doesn't say anything to make me feel stupid about this whole thing.

"It makes sense," he says with relief. I'm not relieved, I'm nervous.

"Right," I say.

"We need to speak to your Alice," he says.

"She isn't mine; I only know her name."

"If we've seen her, surely she lives here. Maybe we can ask around." He signals Hannah to come over.

"Is everything okay?" Hannah asks, her brow frowning.

"Do you know someone, a woman, like a clairvoyant, that lives in this village?" I ask quickly, realising how ridiculous I sound.

"No, love. We don't have anyone like that. According to the myths in the books, our folk didn't think too much of them and they were mostly burnt in the 1500s. Everyone here knows everyone," Hannah says. She sees my expression and her eyebrows curve inwards. "Are you sure you are okay?"

"No," I choke out, shaking.

I have goose bumps, and even Harry's face looks paler. Who the fuck is the woman on the TV and how has no one seen her? How have we seen her? We nearly ran her over.

"I'm only over here if you need anything," she says, putting her arm around my shoulder and then leaving me to Harry.

Harry drapes his jacket around my shoulders, and I pull it tightly around me.

"What the fuck's going on?" I whisper to him. Harry bites his lip.

Hannah must think we are absolutely bonkers.

"I don't know. Maybe she keeps to herself and no one knows her," he says.

"But we've seen her shopping," I persist.

"Surely there is a phone book with all the residents in it," Harry says.

Of course, there would be. Maybe she does just keep to herself. Maybe she doesn't get out much? Or she could just be a visitor over Christmas.

We both put money down on the table and leave a little extra for Hannah, who's watching us leave and frowning.

We stand out in the cold air. The sky is threatening to rain again and puddles dot the paths.

Glenda is power walking towards us, her heels

clicking on the stone pavement.

"What are you both doing standing out here? You'll catch your deaths." She says.

"We just had breakfast at Hannah's," I say.

I loop my arm through Harry's and Glenda notices.

"Oh, well, that's good. The old girl is getting a little forgetful these days." Glenda shakes her blonde bob, making it bounce.

"Glenda, can we ask something?" I say, and Glenda encourages us to 'walk and talk' because she has to get to the museum and we can come along too if we want.

"What is it, dear?" she asks, straightening her mirror. She starts the car as the rain slides down the window.

"Is there a mystic person on the island?"

"Mystic?" she asks with a frown.

"A clairvoyant," Harry adds quickly, and for a brief second, I feel like she's going to open up to us. My entire body tenses, but then Glenda lets out a nervous laugh.

"A clairvoyant? Of course not," she says.

"Was there anyone that lived here called Alice?" I ask.

"No, dear." She shakes her head, driving us to the museum. I look at Harry, who shrugs unhelpfully.

Well, what the fuck do we do now?

"Was there ever anyone on the island that could see the future?" Harry asks.

"Yes, there would have been a long time ago. I

think they're a special clan of their own and they mostly kept to themselves. My great grandma said that people used to sneak to their houses to get their palms read." The windscreen wipers screech as Glenda pauses.

"Of course, back then, you had to be careful, because if any authority thought you had magic powers, they would burn you at the stake. The islanders were nervous about any kind of magic after the myth of the fairy flag. I'm sure you know all about that," she says. Me and Harry look at each other and Glenda continues. "After the third call was made, the islanders suspected the fairies were sending someone onto the island to help kill the chiefs. Anyone clairvoyant would have been viewed as someone sent from the fairies with dark magic and therefore would have been chased out or killed," she says.

"Glenda, have you ever had anything happen to you that you just can't explain?" I blurt out, not meaning to, but I just can't contain it. The more I hear about clairvoyants and fairies, the more I'm itching to get to the museum and hopefully find something that helps us.

"Of course, dear." She smiles as we park up. "The fairies are looking down on us all. They look after their own, you know. If something is going on, they'll be behind it. They see everything and only bring together the really special ones. True love means everything to them," she says.

The only sound is coming from the tapping of the rain on the windows and the rhythmic wipers scraping on the window. Rog is wrapped up in a blanket on the back seat in between Harry and me.

"How did you meet your husband?" I ask.

"Well, now, that was forty years ago. Joe was a farmer on the land. One day, I was walking my dog, and he started growling profusely at this little hut. As I got closer, I noticed a barely conscious man. I ran back to the farmhouse where Joe's dad lived. Within minutes, they had him in the car on the way to the hospital. The nurses said if he'd been left ten minutes more, he would have died."

"That's so sad," I say, a lump rising in my throat.

"That isn't all, though. My parents were new to the island. They were property developers and wanted to buy land for houses, but there was a huge argument between our families and it drew us apart. We were forbidden to see each other," she says.

"So what happened?" Harry asks.

"It's a little fuzzy now, but the strangest thing happened to stop the land being sold... and my parents divorced, and I managed to stay all these years. I can't remember exactly." She shakes her head as if trying to get the memories back.

"But you knew you should be together?" I say.

"Exactly. It was like fate itself was giving us a push in the right direction."

◆ ◆ ◆

The air is cold and damp and my shoes will get soaked if we stay out here. Not that I care that much. I wish we could push Glenda to remember. Surely that wasn't all. Hannah hinted Glenda had an experience like we were having. Maybe she has to be quiet about it or is she worried about history repeating itself?

How does all of this fit in with us? I still don't understand what exactly is going on. I know we both feel the same way now, but we just can't seem to get over the invisible line.

Glenda offers us a drink, but I decline. I don't want to be locked in the café again. We need to look around. Surely, if anyone knows where a clairvoyant might have lived back in the day, it's here at the same castle that holds the cloth of the fairies and the horn of the chief.

I think back to *round and round*. Is it somewhere in the castle? What is round and round here? I look towards the grounds and the well-attended lawn. It isn't round, so that's not helpful. If fate wants us to figure this out, I wish fate had made it a bit easier than this.

"What do you want to do here?" Harry asks, holding Rog's lead as we wait for him to finish doing his business.

"Harry, what could they have meant by round and round?" I ask, thinking out loud.

"I haven't the foggiest," he says and shakes his head.

"One thing though," I whisper, and he leans closer to me while Glenda is sorting out something in the boot of her car.

"What?"

"Let's not get fucking locked in that café," I say, and he laughs.

◆ ◆ ◆

The grand reception is absolutely beautiful. The hall has a pristine carpet that looks like it's been rolled out especially for us, like we're VIPs, only it isn't the customary red but a deep shade of royal blue. I love this place. I can't describe the feeling I get stepping into it, knowing it's a place where the chiefs lived. A piece of history. I feel fulfilled, almost giddy.

At the end of the entrance is a grand staircase. It's immaculately kept. Peter must be amazing at keeping up on the maintenance.

"Where to?" Harry whispers next to me.

Why do I have such a strong gut feeling about being here? It's like the universe is pulling me in this direction and I need to be at the castle for whatever reason.

"I don't know?" I say, my voice echoing in the vast corridors. Each beautifully carved wooden door leads to another piece of history.

"Maybe we should get a map from the gift shop," Harry suggests.

"Yes," I say and follow him along the corridor to

where a line of tourists are involved on a tour of the castle.

We follow the signs to the gift shop. At the front near the till is a stack of maps. I recognise Joe. "Hello, welcome to our gift shop," he greets us.

"Hi." I smile and take a map. Joe taps it into the till and we pay.

The map is like a scroll folding out to show us the layout of the castle.

"Right." Harry opens the scroll and stretches it out. It's covered in swirling, neat handwriting.

"Round and round," I repeat in my head, looking at the map for any clue. Nothing makes sense, but it has to mean something.

"Why don't we start upstairs and work our way down? We can just have a brief look around," Harry says.

We return to the reception with the grand staircase. A few centrepieces of history are on stands around the room and I glance over them.

"If we go upstairs, there are some bedrooms." Harry points to one bit of the map. "It says here the rooms coloured in are the ones out of bounds, so we won't be able to check there." At the top of the stairs, a long corridor lined with wooden doors stretches before us. "These are out of bounds." He indicates the left wing.

The first room we go to looks like an old sitting room with a golden framed photo of the chief clan on the wall.

I move closer to it. The clan look in mid-celebration for something.

I'm searching the picture for any clues, but I can't figure it out. Even Harry steps closer to have a look.

"Nothing," he says and shakes his head.

The rest of the room looks ordinary. An old bookshelf towers high, full of books similar to the ones in the attic. They're all about the history of the castle and the island.

"Could they be a clue?" Harry asks as I'm reading the spines of the books. Some of them look like they date back hundreds of years, but they are all in immaculate condition.

"I doubt it." I pull one out that's a tourist guide to the fairy pools. The pages inside are delicate and slightly discoloured, but the book isn't coming apart at the spine like I expected.

I read over the history of the pools, beginning with how they were formed. It might not solve the mystery, but it's fascinating. A hand-drawn illustration shows how a volcano erupted, forming the pools in their perfect position beneath the towering Cuillins. There's so much more to them than just a tourist spot. They're history. Their very foundation is like a living soul, an enchanted heartbeat where the magic originates and disperses across the island.

Every new fragment of information plays with my imagination. The history looks black and white on paper, but the myths and legends weave through it, painting it with fascinating colours and leaving shiny trails of fairy dust just waiting to be followed. Is this why the islanders trust the myths and believe they'll find their soul mate?

Before we came here, I would have laughed at the idea of a soul mate. But now? I'm not so sure.

Who wants Harry and me to spend so much time together and get so close in this adventure? And why? If we're supposed to go our separate ways after, then it doesn't make sense. But can we be destined to live on this island together?

All I know is the idea of going home and leaving Harry to live here without me cuts like a shard of glass between my ribs and I can't bear it.

"Look here," Harry shouts from a chair in the corner of the room by the window next to where Rog has curled up on the floor. I return my book and Harry shuffles to let me sit down.

He flips through a dusty book and the page falls open on one of the clan chiefs. The portrait is similar to the one on the wall.

"Look at this." He flicks a few pages, landing on a lady with long brown hair.

Alice MacGausty, the caption reads.

I read through the pages. She's the chief's only daughter, after his wife died giving birth to her.

"We've found Alice," he whispers, looking up for my reaction.

"But this is in the fifteen hundreds," I say, confused.

"I know," he says, and a shiver runs up my spine.

"She was one of the last people in Scotland to be burnt at the stake." Harry shows me the illustration of what it would've been like. She's tied to a plank of wood with rope all over her body.

"Shit," I say and swallow the lump in my throat.

"Are you okay?" he asks and I lean my head on him. He kisses it softly.

"Why is there nothing else about her anywhere?" I scan around. "What has that got to do with what she said? Round and round?"

I'm more confused than before. The girl I've been seeing is dead. What does that say about me?

"I don't know," he says, putting the book back. A noise comes from the bookshelf.

We both step backwards as the machinery or mechanics inside turn. When they're quiet, Harry pulls on what would be the door and it opens into a stone staircase like the one that leads down to the café. Rog comes trotting over curiously.

A tiny window opposite illuminates the top few steps of a downward staircase before it spirals into darkness.

"This isn't creepy at all," Harry jokes and I smile.

Curiosity gets the better of me and I can't help wanting to go and have a look. Rog is already halfway down.

"No, Rog, we don't have a torch." Harry pats his knees and Rog comes back.

The sun is going down. How long have we been

searching the castle for?

"We have to do this, Harry. It could be our way out." I take another step towards it.

"Em, we can come back early in the morning. One more day won't do us any harm." He holds my arm to stop me from going any further.

"What about Claire and her dad? You can't just give up your job and break up with her again," I say, irritated.

"I would though, for you," he says.

"Harry," I start, and he puts his hand up to stop me from talking. The sun casts a shadow on his face.

"Em, I know we haven't always seen eye to eye and I will be forever making it up to you."

"I was so confused." I shake my head, remembering the day. It was horrible seeing him flirting with someone else whilst we were still together.

"I knew it was wrong, but I didn't know what to do, and it turns out she's a controlling cow trying to take me away from my friends," he says.

"Karma," I say with a smile.

"But since we've come here and spent so much time together, I feel like this time-loop- experience has brought us together and shown us what we kept throwing away was worth keeping."

"Are you going to move here?" I ask. The shard of glass is cutting deeper into my chest.

"Yes. Are you going to move with me?"

"What about work? What about our home lives,

our homes? " I ask, casually.

"For one, I don't have a job to go back to and my house is owned by Claire," he says.

"Why did you ever think that was a good idea?" I ask. "Along with the bloody tweed and hair gel."

Today, Harry is sporting his collared t-shirt and hoodie, his hair is combed normally and he looks exactly like him.

"I know." He says with a smile, looking at me intensely.

"You never answered my question," he says.

"Yes," I say without thinking about it. Fuck, how are we going to support ourselves?

Harry pulls me into his arms. "Emilia Westbrooks, I fucking love you," he says, and we kiss.

CHAPTER 32

I'm happy. No scrap that. I'm floating along on a cloud. I'm really confused about everything, but the thought of coming back here fills me with so much joy. Holding hands, we trace our way down the stairs where the moonlight is shining onto the floorboards. It looks magical.

The rain outside has died down to a drizzle and we step outside.

"I want to show you something," he whispers, and we sit on the front step together. The drizzle calms me, but it's still cold.

"There you are." Glenda stands with her arms crossed by her car and I've never been so pleased to see her. I rush down the stairs and hug her.

"Thank you," I say, and she stumbles backwards

"Hello, Glenda," Harry says with a smile and opens the car door for me.

"I'm so pleased you both had a good time." Her eyes flash. Why is she in such a good mood?

I sometimes sense she can see through me, which is ridiculous. Well, maybe not. If a few weeks ago somebody had told me what I'd be doing this Christmas, I would have told them they were nuts, but now nothing is impossible.

"Can you stop here, please?" Harry says as we turn onto the swirly road that leads back to Portree.

"Of course. Will you be joining us for the carolling?" she asks

"I'm not sure," Harry says, taking my hand and helping me out of the car. Rog jumps out after me.

We're standing in front of a row of little terraced cottages.

"What are we doing?" I put my hood up.

"I want to show you this cottage. Well, the outside of it at least," he says.

A for sale sign is stuck in the ground by the front door.

"Are you going to buy it?" I spin to face him. His face breaks into a smile.

"I'm thinking about it."

"But surely it must cost a fortune." I don't want to burst his bubble. We aren't rich, though.

"It doesn't. Em, we could start our new life here," he says with a smile and his eyes look so wide. I can't break his heart and remind him to be realistic. Instead, I just nod.

"I was thinking, if after tomorrow we aren't out of this loop, we should try to get in for a showing," he says.

"Yes," I say, and we walk hand in hand, swinging

them slightly as we make our way up the hill to the Inn Keeper.

"You made it then." Annie fusses Rog, who is sniffing by her feet.

"Of course," I say, and she hands me a drink. Razor and Tammy come over.

"We thought something had happened to you," Tammy says with a wink.

"What, outside?" I joke.

"Sure, why not?" she says. I can see she's dying to ask questions about Harry and me, and I'm not sure how to answer her.

"Because we would die of frostbite," I say, and she laughs.

"Yes, because that's the reason," she says.

"Is Claire here?" I ask.

"Nope." Annie appears with Peter wrapped around her.

"Oh," I say, surprised.

I look over to where she would normally sit, and she isn't there.

"She's waiting out back for 'daddy'," she whispers.

I look out of the window and see her sitting on the bench with her bright pink fluffy coat.

"She's been a pain in the arse all night. Blaming us for their breakup," Tammy whispers.

"Can we ditch the carolling?" I don't feel like standing outside in the rain knocking on people's doors.

"What did you want to do?" Tammy asks.

"Get absolutely pissed," I say.
"Amen to that," Annie cheers.

❖ ❖ ❖

"There's a fucking jukebox in the corner!" Razor exclaims, drunkenly.

Everyone has left but us. We are sitting in a little booth near the crackling fire. It seems like no one else wants to go carolling either.

"OMG, can we listen to 'Bob the Builder'?" Annie asks.

I laugh because it's so Annie. As she sings 'Bob the Builder' whilst doing 'big fish little fish' dance moves.

Peter also laughs. "You chose her," I say to him and he laughs again.

"She's great, really," he says and blushes.

"And if you hurt her, you've got us to answer to," Tammy adds.

"Can I get everyone's attention?" Harry asks, and we all go quiet except for 'Bob the Builder' playing in the background. "Well, I want to propose a toast," he starts, and Annie elbows me, raising her eyebrows.

I shove her. "Shut up."

"To Emilia and myself. We're hoping to move here after Christmas." He holds up his pint glass.

"So, you're back on?" Annie asks.

"Yes," we both say together, and everyone cheers.

"This is a cause for celebration," Tammy says,

ordering us more drinks.

"It's about fucking time," Annie says.

"That's great, mate." Razor slaps him on the back. Harry squeezes my hand.

"Excuse me for a second." He nods toward Claire and her dad.

"You don't have to do it right now, Harry," I say, holding his arm.

"For you, I will," he whispers, sending shivers down my spine.

"Pass me the sick bucket." Annie makes puking noises.

Harry walks over to the bar where Claire and her dad are sitting. We turn on our seats and watch. Harry stands confidently while talking to Claire's dad. Razor is on guard in case he tries to hurt him.

"All done." Harry brushes his hands together.

"Really?" I ask, looking at him for any bruises or anything. Was it really that easy?

"You have some explaining to do, Claire Marie Davis." Claire and her weedy-looking dad walk up to us. Claire is staring at her feet. "IIarry, I'm so sorry," he says and they shake hands. My mouth is on the floor.

They leave and we are all staring at Harry. "What?" he asks casually.

"Why the fuck is he shaking your hand?" I ask.

The last time they met, it was less than pleasant. They hated each other and Claire's dad blacklisted him.

"Because I told him the truth of what Claire's been doing," he says.

"What did she do?" Tammy asks.

"The pregnancy test," Annie says, and Tammy gasps.

"She faked it, so I would move in with her and marry her. She told her dad too, so he would give me a raise," he says.

"Shit, man," Razor says.

"It's a good job the fairies were here to bring you two together," Tammy says and we all laugh and toast again to the fairies.

"Any music requests?" Annie asks, flicking through the songs.

Tammy suggests 'Man-eater' by Nelly Furtado, and I giggle.

"Ooh, what about 'Thorn in My Side' by Eurhythmics?" I suggest.

Harry rolls his eyes. "Ha, ha funny, guys." He kisses me whilst the rest of the group whoop and cheer.

I put my arms around him and we sway, even though everyone else is still arguing about the music.

"So, did her dad really let you go scot-free?" I ask, and he nods.

"Yes. I also have a reference from him to apply for a mortgage." He twirls me as 'I've Had the Time of my Life,' by Bill Medley and Jennifer Warnes comes on.

"For the cottage?" I ask, trying not to get excited.

"For the cottage," he repeats, and I can't help but beam. Everything seems to be coming together for us. We just need to get out of this bloody loop.

We move out of the way as Peter and Annie prepare to do the lift.

Oh god!

The room is silent as Annie runs to Peter. Razor gets behind in case Peter drops her, but he keeps her in the air. His arms are shaking and his face is red as she falls off him onto the floor.

"I'm okay," she says, holding up her empty glass. Its contents are all over Razor and Peter.

"Well, that could've gone better," Peter exclaims, helping her up and wrapping his arms around her.

The carollers come back into the Inn Keeper chatting.

"I want to go back," I say into Harry's ear and we call for Rog.

♦ ♦ ♦

Back in our favourite place, we make our way to our balcony hand in hand and lay out our blankets underneath the moon. The drizzly rain has made the air smell fresh and when I look up at Harry, all I see is lust. The funny thing is when we are scrambling to get each other's clothes off; I don't feel anything but love for this man. There is no remorse or regret any more because he is finally mine and we've nearly broken the spell to live the rest of our lives together.

CHAPTER 33

I sit up again next to Harry. I'm dressed and way too warm to still be wrapped around Harry's body.

"Morning," Harry whispers and sits up. Rog is lying on my feet at the end of the bed.

"We are back at in the attic," I say.

"Hopefully for the last time," he says, taking my hand and making me shiver against his touch.

I pick up my phone. The same two texts are on there and the day is still the sixth of December.

Today we will break the loop and then we can carry on with our lives and move into the cottage together.

"Isn't it weird that no one will remember last night?" I say.

"I remember it." He pulls me onto his lap and wraps the quilt around me.

"I will never forget it," I say against his chest, and he kisses my head.

Being able to spend Christmas with Harry is something I think about a lot. I can't wait to wake up and not know what is going to happen.

"Me neither," he says.

"I miss the surprise of the next day and even the damn weather," I say.

"I want to get on with our lives together too, but I don't think I'll ever really make it up to you for leading you on and hurting you."

"Harry, you've done so much for me."

"Well, it just doesn't feel like enough," he says with a sigh.

"We're going to have an amazing life here," I say. I can't wait to live here. I want to visit the castle all the time.

Who actually knows what caused this stupid loop? It's been days now, and I want us to be together forever.

"I know," he says and smiles.

We stumble to get dressed in the dark and head downstairs to the kitchen. Sure enough, the rain is coming down, and Annie is standing by the kitchen in her nightdress. Rog follows us downstairs.

"Is there loads of money up there or something?" Annie asks again, handing us both coffee and eyeing us up suspiciously.

"No," Harry says, and kisses me in a way you wouldn't kiss someone in front of your friends.

"You two are-" she squeals.

"Yes," we say.

"OMG, since when?" Annie's eyes are on us like an excited dog. I can tell she wants to ask us everything, but I can hear Claire moving around the bedroom.

"Last night," I say. There's absolutely no reason to confuse her.

"Ew, I don't need to know the details." She covers her ears, but she's beaming. "So, how did your night go?" I ask.

"It was amazing," she brags. "Peter stayed over last night."

"We heard," Harry interrupts

"No, you didn't." She slaps him playfully. "Do you want to see a photo of his ding-a-ling?" she asks.

Harry does a spit take of his coffee and excuses himself to take Rog outside.

"Go on then, show me," I say and laugh.

Annie gets a picture on her phone and shows us. We erupt in fits of giggles.

"What's so funny?" Claire emerges from the bedroom and Harry walks back in.

"Oh, it's just a rare Scottish animal," I say.

Annie and I burst into giggles again.

"Really?" Claire looks interested.

"Oh yes, the Dragopenis," she says.

Even Harry is struggling to keep a straight face. Meanwhile, Claire looks deadly serious.

"Oh, I have never heard of that," she says, confused.

"Oh, it only comes out at night," Annie says. I have tears in my eyes.

"Is it cute?" she asks.

"Fucking beautiful," Annie says and giggles.

Tears are streaming down my face.

Annie turns the phone to her, and she looks like she is about to throw up.

"That's not beautiful." She shrieks, embarrassed.

We giggle and she strops off.

"I think it's beautiful." She winks at me and I laugh.

Harry wraps his arms around my waist and whispers: "Never show Annie a photo of my dick." I laugh.

We sit in the kitchen in comfortable silence as we finish our drinks.

"So, what are you doing today?" she asks, breaking the silence.

"We're going to the castle," I say, feeling smug, like we are the only ones who know the secret. I'm buzzing with excitement.

"Of course you are." She rolls her eyes.

"I want to know all about you two. Well, maybe not everything," she says.

I shrug.

"We realised how stupid we're being," he says.

"Exactly." I smile.

It's true, and now it feels like everything is coming into place. We just need to get out of this damn loop. We can't buy a house or anything until we do, and if I'm honest, it feels like our lives are stuck. Our happily ever after, if you believe in that, can't happen because of this huge barrier in our way. I really hope today will be the last day of the sixth of December and maybe tomorrow we'll wake up to the ground being covered in snow. Or even a sunny day with no rain and different festivities because I don't want to go fucking carolling again.

"I'll be back in a moment." He kisses me before going into the bedroom he shares with Claire.

"What's he doing?" Annie asks.

"Telling Claire where to go," I say, not sure if I should be hovering around the door listening to their argument.

I hear Claire tell Harry about the baby.

"Oh yeah, I want to show you something." Annie pulls me into the bathroom. "Look." She pulls a badly messed-up pregnancy test out of the bin.

I pretend to be shocked as Annie holds it up and says, "Now, I know this isn't yours."

"No, it isn't." I shake my head.

"Should we tell Harry?" she asks.

"I think it would be better if I do," I say, but she isn't listening. Claire is sitting at the kitchen table trying to talk to Harry. He looks relieved to see us.

"What the fuck is this?" Annie holds up the badly drawn pregnancy test and Claire goes red.

"Urm." Claire looks down at her hands.

"What the fuck, Claire?" Harry says, playing along.

"I urm," she stutters.

She has nothing to say.

"You could have at least made it look real," Annie says.

"So you are definitely not pregnant?" Harry says.

"No," she bursts into tears. "But I feel like you're going to leave me, so I had to do something."

Annie is making cuckoo sounds.

"This is all your fault." She points to me. "You've taken him away from me,"

"I haven't done anything," I protest.

"No, she hasn't. We were going to move in together. What the fuck were you going to do when it was time to give birth?" he yells. "When were you going to tell me the truth?"

"I... don't know," she sobs.

"Does your dad know?" he asks, already knowing the answer. Claire doesn't answer.

"Get the fuck out of here," he yells, making her jump.

Harry pulls me closer to him and sits me on his lap.

"Nice acting," I whisper.

"Thank you," he says and kisses my cheek.

"Fucking hell, that's enough drama for one day," Annie says, getting her coat on to leave.

"Can we go now?" I ask, and he nods. We stand up and get ready as Connie pops her head around the door.

"Hello everyone," she says cheerfully. "I just want to let you know about the carolling later." She stops when she sees Claire and whispers, "We will be in the Inn Keeper at five if you want to join us." She leaves us to it.

"Maybe see you later, yes?" Annie asks and blows

us kisses.

CHAPTER 34

We turn the Christmas radio on and sing badly to the festive tunes as the rain pelts against the window.

The instrumental to 'Last Christmas' by Wham comes on as we park up outside of the castle.

"Torches?" I remind him.

"Check." He salutes me and I giggle. He takes my hand and we walk to the hall.

We follow the map up the spiral stairs and across the corridor into the sitting room. I let Rog off of his lead to go and explore.

The room is undisturbed.

"I could live in this room." I sigh with the biggest smile on my face.

"I know." He smiles when he looks at me, and I feel the butterflies in my stomach.

"Let's get out of this loop," Harry says and squeezes my hand.

We walk to the bookshelf. Rog stands in front of it, barking and growling.

"Come on, Rog." I say and clip the lead on.

Harry presses the button and we walk down

another set of stairs, but this time there's a tiny light from the sun coming through the window.

Harry passes me a torch and we turn them on, going slowly down the steps.

I feel around the wall for a switch and flick it on.

The room lights up. It's a showroom. The walls have many portraits hanging around and, in the middle of the room, in a box, is a chief horn.

Why has this room been locked to the public? It's full of history.

"It's just a normal room." I look around, feeling disappointed.

"Is it?" Harry turns our torches off and we leave them by the door.

"Seems like it," I huff out.

"Have you looked at all the portraits?" he asks.

"No," I say, looking at the first one on the far wall. It's an oil painting of the Fairy Pools. I can't see anything in the painting that looks out of place.

"Em, come here," Harry says from the far end of the room. A table and chairs are going the full length of the room.

He's standing in front of a gold-framed painting of a beautiful woman. Alice. She's draped in brown cloth with what looks like rope tied to her feet. She sits on a small chair.

"This would've been moments before she died," Harry says. He lifts his hand to the painting but doesn't touch it. I don't think we are supposed to touch it.

"Wow," I say, feeling the sadness for her, but

completely confused. "Can you see anything in the painting that might help us?"

Harry reads the description at the bottom *1600 Alice MacGausty in place to be burnt at the stake*

"I can't see anything," I say and sigh.

Why have we found this room if it's not helpful? I was so sure this castle had the answers and now I feel defeated. We really will be stuck in this loop forever.

Harry fiddles around the back of the painting and I watch him as he shines his torch in there. There's something there and I get a sense of hope. Why would something be hidden?

We are careful not to move the painting as I help Harry gather up a really old piece of paper and a diary-type book that's falling apart. Could this be what we are looking for?

CHAPTER 35

"She must've kept a diary," I say. We sit cross-legged on the floor with Rog.

The diary is almost transparent. I don't want to touch it in case it rips. The pages are written in extremely neat handwriting and at the top of the pages are the dates and times the entries were written.

I start flicking through. "Do you think this might be it?" I ask, stopping on a page and reading.

"I'm not sure," he says. He starts reading the page. I put the diary between us to read together. It was written at various stages of Alice's life.

I finish reading an entry where she talks about how her mum died and I swallow down tears.

I wipe my eyes. This is too much now. "It's okay." Harry puts his arms around me and I instantly feel stupid.

"Why is history so sad?" I ask.

"Back then they wouldn't have had medicines for even the simplest of diseases," he says. I nod.

He flicks further through the diary and stops.

"Here's where she was accused," he says, reading it out.

Date 1598

Father is keeping me well hidden. I have developed something that nobody else would understand. He told me someone is looking for me. I don't know who it is, but I'm scared. I'm not allowed out of my bedroom. I can see things, unexplainable things about the future. One of them terrifies father. It's about a beautiful woman coming to our island. All I know is my father likes her. Father is terrified of liking anyone else apart from my mother. That's why I think he has locked me here.

Alice

I listen with tears in my eyes. She must have been so scared. I dread to think about what she would write next.

"Do you want me to carry on?" he asks and I nod. I don't, but I don't want to be in this loop forever. I brace myself for what's coming.

"She must've been a poet or a writer." He flicks through the pages.

"Why?" I ask.

"Because she writes poems for a few pages. Oh, hang on, I think one of them is a folk hymn," he says, passing it to me.

"Round and round," I whisper, seeing the words in the diary, and another shiver courses down my back. Shit. This is seriously creepy.

I'm shaking now. Surely this can't be an enormous coincidence? Does this mean something? I read the neat lines of the poem to the last line.

Keep him safe from harm, cuddle him, comfort him in warmth, and let him know you love him.

I can't stop the tears from falling as I finish reading the page.

"Brace yourself," he says and flicks to the last page.

"1600. Fourth of July," he starts.

The date on the painting of Alice. The day she died.

I wipe my eyes with my sleeve and listen to Harry.

"Dear diary,

I'm scared. They've found me, and in a short while, I will be burnt to death. God, my saviour will be by my side to comfort me but I'm terrified. Father has given me a piece of jewellery my mother owned and told me comforting words about her. Father tried so hard to help me, but after I told him about the beautiful woman coming to see him, he got a little angry. I hope she brings him comfort and joy again when I'm no longer here.

Alice"

He finishes and I can't help the sobs escaping from me. Those last moments before she died must have been terrifying for her.

I stand up and read the description of the painting again.

"How have we seen her here, then?" I ask, wiping my eyes and feeling confused. Alice was at the church sale, the shopping centre, and the pub. We nearly ran her over - and how did I see her on the

TV? Was I drunker than I thought I was?

"None of this makes sense." I shake my head, confused.

"Let's see if her dad is on the wall." Harry takes my hand and we move around the room. All the portraits are of past chiefs and their children. The one in the far corner of the room looks like Alice. The description says:

1540 – 1620 Donald MacGausty,

"Yes. Who is the beautiful woman Alice told him he would see, though?" Harry asks, confused.

"I don't know. There are no more diary entries," I say.

"Could it be a fairy?" he asks, and I feel like everything may have just clicked into place.

"The baby with the cloth?" I add.

We look around the room at the stand. It has the fairy cloth inside it and the date was ten years after Alice died. I look at the piece of almost rotting fabric in the enclosed box and realise how special it is to the history of the island. If none of it is real, then how did this piece of fabric end up here?

"Is that the actual cloth?" he asks.

"I think so. It wouldn't be here otherwise," I say and read the inscription. It's the same poem as Alice wrote in her diary.

"Look, Harry." I point to the poem.

"It's Alice's poem."

"Yes, and look, it says at the bottom, money doesn't always mean everything." I think about when I saw Alice, and she said exactly that to me.

How insane does this all sound?

"She was trying to tell you all along," he says.

"I guess she was," I say. "This whole thing is creepy."

I don't know if I want to find out anything else. What if her body is in here? Did I imagine seeing Alice on the TV? I've seen her four times during my stay here, and technically, it has only been a few days, but with the loop, it feels like we've been stuck here forever.

"Do you think this is it? Could this be the loop breaker?" I ask.

"Maybe," he says, looking at me hopefully and we kiss.

"We're together," I shout into the room and it echoes back to me. "We realise our mistake."

The door handle pulls and we both shriek. Rog stands up barking.

"There you are." Glenda appears at the door, making us jump.

"Yes," we say, flabbergasted.

Shit, are we in trouble?

"Have you found what you were looking for?" She nods towards the diary.

"Um," I say.

"I know," she says at last. "Let's go down to the café and we can talk. And bring the diary."

I quickly put it in my pocket, feeling strange. This isn't what I expected at all. Was Glenda in on this the whole time?

CHAPTER 36

We sit in the same café we've been locked inside on prior days. Rog sniffs under the table for any scraps.

"This is creepy," I whisper.

"It is, but at least she won't lock us in this time," he says.

"Two coffees?" Glenda asks, before putting them in front of us and throwing Rog a sausage under the table.

"Thank you," I say, and smile uncomfortably.

"So let's get straight into this," Glenda says, putting her hands together and my blood runs cold. I hold Harry's hand.

"Okay," I say nervously.

"I'm sorry you've had to go through what you have," she says.

"Can we ask something?" I ask.

"Of course," Glenda puts down her cup.

"Did you go through this?"

"We're all friends here, aren't we?" she asks, looking around. It's like she's paranoid that someone else is listening.

"Of course," Harry reassures her. We're waiting

for her to carry on with bated breath.

"I haven't spoken about it in nearly fifty years," she whispers.

"So, has this happened before?" I ask again.

"Yes. Someone was really watching over you two when they decided you belonged together." She smiles. "It's definitely a blessing."

"We didn't realise how stupid we've been," Harry says. "Em, I'm truly sorry for breaking us up." I squeeze his hand.

"This island is meant for people who are in love. Haven't you noticed we're all oldies here?" she says, sipping her tea.

"That's not true," I say.

"We've been on this island for generations. My parents married here and now I'm married and I hope Peter gets married here one day," she says.

"So, is it only native people that believe they stay together?" Harry asks.

"Of course not. The islanders believe that if it's true love, then the fairies will help you realise that. That's what has happened to you two. You didn't take as long as Joe and I did, though. We didn't figure it out for... Well, ages." She sighs. I feel uneasy again.

"How long exactly?" I ask.

I couldn't imagine being in this loop for much longer. I want to live my life with Harry.

"A year," she whispers.

"Wow," I say.

"Did you read this diary?" I ask curiously.

"Yes," she says.

"I have photocopies of it somewhere at home. I keep it locked up. It's our secret."

"So no one else on the island has been through this?" Harry asks.

"We don't know. We don't talk about it. I imagine they may have. Alice seemed very strong-willed and something in her made me think of you," she says, putting her hand over mine.

"She was beautiful," I say.

I still feel like I've invaded her privacy by reading her diary.

"She was. It's really sad how it all ended." Glenda dabs her eyes with a handkerchief.

"I'm still confused about all of this," Harry says and shakes his head.

"Emilia told me she first saw Alice on TV, but how can that be? I also saw her on the TV?" Harry asks.

"The answer is, I don't know. She might have been on TV, or our subconscious minds dreamt her up," Glenda says.

"I saw her -and so did Lucy and Dan," I say. "I rang the TV and told her everything."

"That was you?" Harry was looking at me, bewildered.

"Yes. I thought you had gone out with Annie and Razor," I say.

"No, I didn't go out for New Year," he says.

I was certain everyone had gone out, and that

was why I stayed behind. Razor and Tammy were all loved up, and Annie would find someone at the club to go home with. I would be left with Harry, and back then, we were still sleeping together.

"I didn't want to face everyone," I say.

"Me neither." He takes my hand and I wonder how our breakups and getting back together have affected him. I've been so selfish just thinking about myself.

"See, everything has worked out for you," Glenda says.

"It has," we both say.

Glenda serves us tea and freshly-made scones on beautiful blue plates.

"I'm sorry for locking you in," Glenda says, and I know at that moment she knew what was going on. She has always known what was going on and I'm not sure if that makes it more or less creepy.

"At least you left the wine," I say.

"Exactly," Harry says, and Glenda laughs.

"So, what are you going to do with your freedom after today?" she asks, and I take a bite out of the best scone I've ever tasted in my life.

"Well, that's the thing," Harry starts. "We want to be a part of the island."

"It's absolutely beautiful here," I agree.

"That it is, and I'm thrilled you want to live here. But I want to know what you want to do?" she asks.

"I'm not sure yet," he says. "I'm going to quit my job tonight and then I want to celebrate." We clink our cups together to toast.

"A little birdie told me Hannah wants to retire from the café," Glenda says and winks. I look at Harry. I think about that little café and the beautiful breakfasts Hannah does. Could I do that? What do I want to do when I'm here?

"I would love to work at the café," I say.

"Well, I wouldn't mind the help around the castle," she says.

I don't mind what job I do when we move here. I've never really felt like I belonged in Mum and Dad's sweetshop. It was just a means to pay the bills until I got my shit together, which never happened. I was just too comfortable and too afraid to step out and do something I might love.

"I don't mind working in the café," Harry says.

"I didn't know you can cook," I say.

He's definitely a dark horse. If you took him at face value, you wouldn't believe half of the things I know about him, and that's only because I've known the man all my life.

"There is a lot you don't know," he says, and I shove him playfully.

"Are you coming to the carolling tonight?" Glenda asks.

"No." We both shake our heads.

I feel the tiniest bit guilty saying no, but I don't want to sing again. I want to celebrate our new freedom, and that's what it is. Not just being out of the loop, but finding something to do in my life that I'm happy about.

Glenda just laughs. "Enjoy your evening and I'll see you later." She winks before gathering everything up to clean.

"What do you want to do now?" I ask.

CHAPTER 37

There's no point staying at the castle. Now we've unearthed the secret we need to get our lives back on track. Harry is fiddling with his keys.

"Why are you nervous?" I ask.

"Because this is the last time I ever have to do this," he says.

"You've done it before."

He kisses me on my cheek as I start the car. Rog is lying on the full length of the back seat.

We slowly drive home, even though the rain has started up with the snow and the road is slushy. I hold my breath as we head down the road where we last saw Alice. I imagine seeing her floating around the road but, as we reach it, it's empty. There's no sign of anyone. Will we ever see her again?

"Harry?" I ask and he turns to me. "Can we do something first?" I guide him to take a detour around the church first. Harry looks at me, confused, as we park up.

The rain is coming down heavier and I pull my

hood over my head.

We get out and walk the short distance to the graveyard. I let Rog off of his lead and let him sniff as I reach Alice's grave. The flowers surrounding the grave are mostly dead. I feel sad. She was such a brave girl who had to go through something unspeakable, and yet no one has kept her grave nice. I'm surprised Glenda hasn't.

I lean down and touch the gravestone. "Thank you," I whisper.

Harry leads us back to the car and then drives into the village.

❖ ❖ ❖

"You're finally here," Annie announces, bending to give Rog some fuss again.

"That we are," I say and smile.

"So, have you had enough suffering from my mum?" Peter jokes.

"We had to escape out of the wall," I say, and Peter laughs.

Peter looks terrified of his mum and I don't blame him. When she wants something, she'll lock two strangers in a room to try to get them together.

"So are you coming to the carolling?" Annie asks.

"No," I say at the same time as Harry. Annie cheers

"Hallefuckingllejah." She goes off to order us drinks.

We sit down at the table as Claire walks in with her dad. Her eyes are puffy and her dad looks concerned.

I know this will be the last time we see either of them again.

"Harry, are you sure you want to do this?" I ask.

"Of course, is something wrong?" he asks, his eyebrows arching inwards.

"No, I just want to make sure it's what you want," I say, and he smiles to reassure me.

"Fucking hell, woman, he's spent half his life trying to get you," Razor teases as he gets closer to the table, with Annie carrying the drinks.

"He's a right soppy git," Annie says, and I laugh, watching Harry redden.

"I'm not that bad," he says.

"You are." Annie echoes the words.

"Thanks, guys," Harry says and they shrug him off with a no problem.

"I think we should toast," I say, changing the subject and taking the heat off Harry.

Everyone puts up their drinks.

"To new lives and new beginnings," I say, and they toast it.

"So, what's happening between you both?" Annie asks, and everyone looks at us.

"We're thinking of moving out here together," I say.

"OMG! That's amazing." Tammy squeals and hugs us.

"It really is guys," Annie says.

"What about you and Peter?" I say, looking at them.

"We're taking it easy. I'm coming up here for holidays," Annie says. I smile at them. I'm so happy for her.

"What about the portrait you have to do?" Harry asks.

Peter reddens. Oh shit, she did it.

"No…" I gasp and she giggles and winks.

"Fucking hell yes," she says, and I clink my glass with her. "It's about time the biddies got to see what I sleep with."

I giggle, imagining the posh older people seeing Peter naked.

"I haven't painted his face. Just his body," she whispers.

"That makes it better," I say.

"At least my mum won't see it," Peter says, and I laugh. I don't think Glenda would be too impressed.

"Excuse me," Harry says. He walks off to see Claire and her dad. I wait for him to come back and when he does, he looks relieved.

"All done, for the last time," he whispers as Claire's dad comes over.

"Harry, I'm sorry to lose you as a hard worker. I wish you all the best." And then he shakes our hands and leaves.

"Whoop, you got rid of the monster." Annie cheers.

"This is a celebration," Tammy says, and she and

Annie walk off to the dance floor.

"Want to dance, Em?" Harry asks, reaching his hand out to me as a slow song comes on the jukebox. I lean against his chest, feeling like everything's all right with the world. I'm feeling peaceful, and I have the man I was always supposed to have.

CHAPTER 38

It's Christmas Eve, and the weather got the memo. It's freezing. I'm grateful for the change of weather and the change of days. It was amazing waking up the day after we broke the loop to sunshine and not having to make yet another excuse why we didn't want to go carolling.

Today, though, we have what Glenda calls the "festival" of Christmas. I'm not sure what it's about.

I've grown to love the villagers of this island so much. Since our time loop, Hannah and Glenda have opened up to us more, and it feels like we're in this little secret that hardly anyone else knows about. Hannah has spoken to us about retiring. She wants to go fishing with Simon, her husband.

"So, what do you think of the house?" Harry interrupts my thoughts.

I'm sitting on the front porch of our almost new home. Rog has his tongue dangling out of the side of his mouth while he sniffs around the grass.

I say almost because we're about to say yes to it. We've already made an appointment with Claire's dad, which will be the weirdest thing ever, but he has promised to see us for a mortgage. I feel like I'm finally growing up and doing adult things. Mortgages and homes are what my parents and older siblings have. The only problem I have is not upsetting my parents by telling them I don't want to work in the sweetshop any more.

"I love it," I say; I smile and sip the flask of coffee Hannah has given us because the electrics aren't working yet and we need a decent drink in us.

We watch the clouds roll over the mountains. I'll never get over the view of the rolling green hills dotted with farm animals and the beautiful grand mountains towering in the distance. I feel like I'm on a postcard.

"Me too." He sits down next to me on the chair and opens up his flask.

Our friends don't seem to mind that we won't see them as often, since the drive up here takes forever. They are happy for us.

I am feeling happy. I didn't imagine I would be potentially working in such an amazing place. Glenda told me to wait until the summer when the Fairy Pools aren't so cold and we can swim in the sea. I'm not sure we'll ever want to go to the Fairy Pools again.

I hear a noise in the distance and see Glenda climbing up the hill and waving her arms at us.

"I hope you don't mind," Glenda shouts as she

gets closer. Behind her, it seems, is most of the village. Are we in trouble?

"Um, no, of course not," Harry answers, biting his lip, which is incredibly sexy.

I wave awkwardly to everyone who's now surrounding us, carrying bags and what looks like plates covered in foil. Rog is in his element as the villagers drop him bits of sausage roll and ham before placing them on the table.

"We thought you might be hungry," Glenda says, like it wasn't a big deal, and my eyes water. They've done all of this for us.

I stand up and walk over to uncover the plates of food that smell amazing.

The plates are full of quiches and sandwiches filled with everything you can think of, plus potato salad and soup in containers.

Tears start to fall.

"We want to welcome you to the island," Hannah says, and I hug her. I can't believe everyone is so kind.

"You're very welcome," Glenda says. Peter comes over holding hands with Annie.

"I'm going to fucking miss you," she says, throwing her arms around me. We cry on each other's shoulders.

"Fuck off, you soppy bitch," I manage to squeak out, and we laugh while wiping our tears.

"Me too." Tammy piles her arms around us and the guys join in.

"Guys, it isn't like we're never going to see you

again," Harry says.

"Exactly," I add.

"We'll have to come and stay with your parents more," Tammy says to Razor, who doesn't look impressed.

"Your parents aren't that bad," I whisper.

"No, I like them," Harry agrees.

"Not as bad as Glenda," Annie whispers and rolls her eyes.

I know Glenda has been very full-on since Peter announced he's going to stay with Annie for a couple of weeks as 'holiday time'. She's been warning him what to pack and asking for her address and even saying she wants to see where Annie lives herself.

I've grown to love Glenda almost like a second Scottish mum, but we know what she's like. We completely understand why her husband and son just agree with her.

"I can't wait to see where you work," Peter says to Annie.

Annie has finally finished her portrait of Peter and it's stacked away in her car, ready to go home with them. We're waiting for her gallery party for the new collection: 'Nature.'

"Me neither," she says and winks.

"We have a lot to celebrate tonight," Harry says.

"We do, but aren't you going to give us a tour first?" Tammy asks.

"I'm freezing my nipples off out here," Annie

says. Peter raises his eyebrows and gets a nudge in his ribs with her elbow.

"Ouch," he complains, and she kisses him.

"Come on then, but don't break anything."

We hold hands and lead them inside.

◆ ◆ ◆

We show off the beautiful living area with the fireplace. I cannot wait to go out and collect the wood for it. The living room leads into the little kitchen that needs flooring and cupboards putting in, but I couldn't resist the ruby red tiles on the wall. I can't imagine anyone pulling them up. We pad up the carpeted stairs and into our bedroom with the ceiling panels and stone feature wall. The entire house is beautiful. I can't imagine anywhere else I'd want to live.

"We will need to have radiators and a boiler fitted," I say, flicking the light switch to show nothing happens. It's already getting darker outside. I see someone attaching a gazebo - in case it rains - out of the window.

"So, what are you doing until you move in?" Annie asks.

"My mum is letting them stay in the cabin," Razor says.

Razor is our legal representative and amazing at his job. He says the house was desperate to be sold. It has a few repair issues, but we can start on those as soon as the Christmas holidays are over.

"That's so cool," Annie says.

"I'm sure we can stay until after the New Year if you want to?" Peter suggests.

"I'd like that," Annie says.

"Hello everyone." Connie comes over full of hugs for all of us.

"Congratulations on the house," she says to us.

"Thank you," we say. Razor comes back.

"The offer was accepted after a little negotiating," he says, and Connie hugs him whilst his cheeks redden.

"Oh, Ranulph," she cries, and he looks away, embarrassed. We all chuckle because we know she is a little overbearing, but she means well.

"Are you coming to the service tonight?" she asks, and lectures Razor on his religion.

"Of course, Mum," he mumbles.

"Yes," we all say. I can't wait to sing the hymns and welcome Christmas. Everyone is coming to the Inn Keeper tonight, including our parents, which makes me a little nervous. We will have to tell them we are moving here. Although, they'll probably be happy we finally sorted our 'modern problems.'

"I'm pleased to hear that." Glenda comes over and Peter gives her a peck on her cheek.

"I can't wait," I say.

"Shall we tuck into the food before it starts raining?" Hannah comes over, holding Simon's hand.

"Yes," I say, feeling my stomach rumble.

We don't have enough chairs for everyone. Some of the little choir singers are practising on the grassy bit of the garden, and fussing Rog who loves all the attention.

"Oh, I almost forgot. We've got something for you." Glenda leaves and returns with fairy lights to drape around the roof of the house. As the men drape the lights on the roof, we watch while we eat up the quiches and sandwiches.

Harry sits down happy with himself when they turn the lights on. The roof of the house lights up in a pale, twinkly white.

"Much better," Glenda says and sits down next to me.

"So, is everything okay?" she asks me. Harry goes over to socialise with the villagers.

"Of course," I say, watching the sun setting in the background.

"You don't get used to it, you know," she says, looking out into the distance.

"It's so beautiful," I say, tucking into a salmon and cucumber sandwich and swigging out of my flask. "I've never been happier."

It's true, I haven't.

"Well, I know that you and Harry looked at each other's notes," she tuts. "But it doesn't matter." She puts her arm on mine. "I'm so pleased you both found what you were looking for on the island."

"Me too," I say.

"So, I want to talk to you about the vacancies

here."

My heart starts thumping.

"Okay," I say for her to go on.

"There's one job at the castle." She bites her lip and I think, *oh god.*

"What?" I ask

"It is a manager role though," she adds, and my heart sinks. I haven't managed anyone in my life. I've never really done anything in my life. I don't know what I'm good at.

"Oh." My face falls, and she senses my disappointment.

"Do you want it?" she asks.

I look over at Harry kicking a football around with a couple of kids.

What will he say to it? Should I ask first? "I would love that," I cry.

I suddenly feel overwhelmed that she would offer this to me, considering I don't know her that well.

"I know you'll do a fantastic job." She hugs me and I catch Harry's eye and gesture for him to come over.

"What?" he asks, looking from me to Glenda.

"She accepted the job." Glenda claps and I look at him, stunned. Did he know? Had he already accepted?

"That's amazing," he says and smiles and I feel small, like they had this secret.

"I have to do some bossing around," Glenda says and leaves us.

"You knew?" I ask.

"Yes, she asked me earlier, and I said I thought you were a better choice for it." He takes my hands, spinning me around and pulling me against him.

"Harry, there are kids around," I whisper as he kisses me.

"Shush," he says, dancing with me even though there isn't any music.

We stay at the house after everyone else has left. I can't believe this place might be ours. It's cold, but I don't want to leave yet.

"Can we stay a little longer?" I ask. Harry has the radio on in the car with the door open, trying to get us to leave, but I don't want to.

"We promised we would show our faces," Harry says and I pout. He laughs.

"We can come back tomorrow," he says, and I nod. I guess that's good enough. It isn't like we can sleep here, anyway. We have no furniture or heating.

I begrudgingly head to the car as Wizzard starts booming through the speakers. We sing along throughout the car journey that's less than five minutes long.

"So, what is happening tonight?" I ask.

"I think Glenda said something about Santa night," Harry says, but I see something in his eyes. What else is going on?

"Go and get changed quickly. You are late." One of the villagers thrusts a costume at Harry and he goes inside. I don't have time to ask what's going on as I'm pulled inside with Rog.

I find the group sitting at the table near the front of a stage.

"What's going on?" I ask Annie, who puts a pint of beer in front of me.

"Sexy Santa," she whispers, and I laugh. Oh shit, this is going to be funny.

"All of the men have joined." Tammy rolls her eyes

"Welcome to our annual Santa contest. Now, ladies, you need to think carefully about who you would want in your bed tonight." She winks at us all and the crowd whoop.

"First up, we have Simon." I see Hannah cheering.

"What can you offer, Simon?" Glenda asks.

"A bloody good night," he shouts into the microphone, making Hannah blush. We laugh as he proceeds to strip to 'Leave Your Hat On' by Tom Jones. When he puts his Santa hat in a place where Santa hats shouldn't go and I feel like I've seen way more of him than I need to.

"Oh god," Annie shrieks.

I'm laughing way too much to say anything and also cringing a little inside while Tammy has completely covered her eyes.

Hannah cheers as he turns around to flash us his bum.

"That was… Eventful," Glenda says brushing her

hair out of her face, clearly embarrassed.

"We also have a treat for you ladies tonight, as we have three Santas joining us. You'll know two of them from the village, one of them left years ago, but now he has come back with his friends and is going to be joining our Santa contest for the evening. They've decided to do a routine each and one altogether. So let me welcome North 51."

We all cheer as the men come out with their fluffy red Santa outfits and start singing 'Stay Another Day' by East 17, quite badly, although the crowds don't seem to mind. I hear the chanting start halfway through: 'take them off, take them off.'

Glenda comes in when they finish. "Now, now, ladies, be patient. They have another act to do." And the crowds quieten down. I look around, hoping Connie doesn't see whatever Razor is going to do because I have a feeling it might scar her for life. And what the fuck is Peter going to do whilst his mum's here?

"First up, is one of our own, Ranulph," Glenda says, and Razor comes back out, but this time he's wearing golden shorts that could rival Kylie's. Tammy cheers, her face red with excitement.

Razor has his Santa hat on his head (thank god) as he walks off the stage whilst 'Please Come Home for Christmas' by Bon Jovi is on. I back my chair away so he can lap dance on Tammy, who's thrilled with the attention. The rest of the crowd is whistling. At the end, he puts his hat on Tammy and winks at her before going back on stage.

"Well, wasn't that… Um, nice?" Everyone claps loudly and I see Tammy down her drink.

"I'll be back," she whispers and goes off to find Razor.

"You don't think Peter would do this, do you?" Annie bites her lip, looking at Glenda, and I laugh. God help his mum if he does.

"I don't know," I say as Glenda introduces a local to the stage who's playing badly on the saxophone.

"I've created a monster," Annie whispers, and I laugh again. She has.

The crowd clap as he walks off the stage bowing. We've gate-crashed the contest and I'm guessing it used to be a lot less dirty than it is now.

"I would like to welcome you to the stage, Fergus." Glenda claps as Razor's dad, who usually doesn't say much, but has been on the booze, comes out. Connie is standing at the bar, her mouth wide open. Fergus's Santa outfit is undone at the front to reveal his red velvet boxers with white around the sides.

"Oh god," I whisper, cringing in my drink. Thank god, Razor is with Tammy.

He sings and dances (badly), grinding on the floor and I can see Connie die of embarrassment. I can't help but laugh the whole time and Annie bites her lip to stop herself as well.

"Where are our men?" Annie shouts

"Yeah," I join in, slightly tipsy. I wonder what Harry and Peter have to show us. Will it be embarrassing? These people are going to be our neighbours. I don't want to forever be known for my boyfriend dancing badly and showing us up.

"Thank you, Fergus." Glenda claps with not much enthusiasm.

"Next up is our 'hot Santa,'" She reads.

I squirm in the chair. Who is the hot Santa? Is it mine or Annie's boyfriend? "Harry Birchwood," Glenda announces. I bite my lip. Harry comes out in just his red Santa trousers and no top. He's carrying sticks that Peter helps light on fire. Oh god, this can only end badly. I cringe with my hand over my eyes. The crowd is cheering him on and Harry juggles sticks on fire whilst dancing to 'Firestarter' by Prodigy. It turns out Harry has a hidden talent. I mean, who knew? I remove my hands from my face and smile as Harry finishes off by blowing on the fire to put it out and removing his trousers and boxers and turning around to reveal his bum. OMG. How much has he drunk?

"Wow, who knew?" Annie says and claps along with everyone else. Harry gets off the stage to get dressed.

"Wasn't that compelling?" Glenda says, pulling on the collar of her shirt.

"Lastly, we have Peter, my son. God bless him." Glenda does the sign of the cross and Harry comes out to sit with me.

"What the fuck was that?" I ask, and he sips his

drink.

"I wanted to show off my skills." He puts his arm around me. I notice he isn't fully dressed.

"Aren't you a lucky girl?" Hannah says as she walks by us

I laugh. I can't believe he did that.

Peter comes on the stage fully dressed and Annie boos him. He gestures for her to come up and she does. He then dances around her whilst getting undressed and shaking his hips around. Annie looks like all of her Christmases have come at once, and Glenda looks like she is about to die. He finishes practically naked and Glenda quickly interrupts before he can take the last part off.

"Thank you, Peter," she says, and her face is blotchy and red. I giggle at her reaction and Harry gives him a massive cheer.

"Well, that was the most fun I think I have ever had," Peter says, sitting down next to Annie, who is still recovering from it all.

"Your mum looks like she is going to pass out," I say to him.

"She'll be fine after a few glasses of sherry," he says and we all toast with our drinks to our new friendship. Peter fits in well with our group and it's a good job because he seems perfect for Annie.

Glenda comes over. "Well, that was eventful, everyone," she says too brightly, with her smile too wide.

"It was great, Glenda," Annie says and lifts her

glass to her.

"To your mum," she says and Glenda's cheeks redden and she bats us all away.

◆ ◆ ◆

The door flings open and half of our families come bounding in. "Hello." I wave to Mum and Dad followed by Harry's mum, who walks through the pub.

"Hi Mum," I say, going red at the attention, and Harry's mum also gives me a sloppy granny kiss.

"Where's Harry?" she asks.

"He's just gone to the loo," I say. Thank god they didn't turn up fifteen minutes ago.

"Is someone going to get me a drink?" Mum asks.

"Where are Lucy and Dan?" I ask.

"They've checked into the hotel. The drive up was crazy," she says.

Harry kissed a cow on the drive up here. I wish I'd videoed it but, back then, things were weird between us. I think back to that and how stupid we were and how it took something massive for us to get together.

Harry gets up to get the drinks and I go with him.

"I'm nervous," I say as we wait at the bar for our drinks.

"Me too. I was excited this morning but now they're here I'm shitting it a little," he whispers.

"Can I help at all?" my mum appears by my side. "Is this a private conversation?" she whispers.

"No, mum but we need to talk," I say and look at Harry.

He nods confidently and smiles at me.

"You two?" She looks between us and we nod slowly.

"It's about time." She cheers and goes off to tell Harry's mum. They've always gossiped about us. But since we were neighbours and best friends, it was probably going to eventually happen.

Harry's mum throws her arms around us both. "Finally," she shrieks.

"That isn't what we want to tell you," I say

They both look at us expectedly. I fiddle with my hands, knowing they're both watching me.

"Mum," I start. "Harry and I are buying a house here."

"Oh, that's great, honey, you've bought a holiday home."

"No," Harry says, clearing his throat. I'm thankful he has taken over talking. "We're moving here," he says.

"But what about your job?" Mum asks and I see the worry lines appear on her face.

"I'm finding something for me to do up here," I say finally.

"Oh," she says and her voice goes quiet.

I feel the guilt stirring around in my stomach and I feel sick.

"I'm sorry, mum but we've had the best time

here," I say and take her hand. It's clammy, and she's shaking.

Dad comes over and sits down. He sees mum's surprised face and looks at us all.

"What's going on?" he asks.

"I'm moving up here, dad," I say.

Dad's face changes from surprised to happy, like a slide-show.

"Oh," Dad repeats Mum's words.

"Our girl's leaving us, David." Mum sobs into her tissue and my gut twists.

Harry squeezes her hand.

"So, Emilia, do you have somewhere to live?" Dad starts with his 'dadisms.'

I hate when he uses my full name. He and Mum are the only ones that have done it since I was ten.

"Yes, dad," I say.

"The house is about ten minutes away from here," Harry says.

"And you two are you..?" Dad asks.

"Yes, dad," I say.

"Well, I am so happy for you both." Harry's mum springs into action and hugs us both.

"It'll be a wonderful new adventure for you both, but you will come and visit, won't you?" she asks.

"Of course," we both say.

We awkwardly hug Harry's mum, but my mum and dad are clearly in shock still.

Mum looks really hurt. Did she think I wanted to stay in the sweetshop forever? Did she want me to stay? I always thought I was in the way.

"Mum?" I encourage her to say something, pretty much anything, because I'm not sure I can take her being upset. The guilt will eat me alive.

"Sorry, love, it's just come out of nowhere," she says and smiles at us both.

"Mum, you know I'll come home as much as I can and, of course, you can stay here with us," I say and she strokes my hair.

"I know, love. You're so grown up now. I should've known this would happen, eventually." She holds me at arm's length. "You look really happy." She hooks her arm through mine. "Any chance of a peep at the house?" she asks and I look to Harry, who nods and gathers up our parents. I clip Rog on his lead, ready to go.

CHAPTER 39

We stay until the winner of the sexy Santa award is announced. Harry wears his sash and Santa hat proudly as we walk out of the Inn Keeper.

"Should I be pleased I missed that?" Harry's mum asks and her cheeks are red. I laugh.

"Probably," I say, feeling pleased his mum missed his little fire juggling, stripping act. The villagers seemed impressed and I'm happy to show Harry off to them. Poor Glenda looked like she was going to have a heart attack seeing Peter.

"So, mum, what do you think?" Harry asks, standing outside the house. The fairy lights are still twinkling on the roof, but the gazebo and everything from earlier is gone.

"It looks lovely," Harry's mum says.

It's cold and we probably shouldn't stay here too long since it's getting dark.

"Can we go inside?" Mum asks me.

"Yes, but we don't have any lighting or heating, so it'll be dark and cold," I warn, and then Harry takes out torches from his pocket.

"I came prepared," he says and takes my hand.

I get excited when we open the door. Every time we come here, I feel at home. I can't wait to live here.

My mum and Harry's mum go and look around upstairs. I take a moment to look out of the window. Now the sun has mostly gone down, it's dark. There aren't any street lights.

"You okay?" I hear Harry's footsteps before he appears. I shine my torch at him.

"Yes," I say. He wraps his arms around me.

"I still can't believe this is ours," I say against his chest

"I know. Both of our parents seem to like it," he says, kissing my hair.

"We should get back soon for the service." I look at my phone screen and realise it starts soon.

Glenda hadn't explained much about tonight. But when she asked us to come along, we agreed straight away. Glenda told us it's a special part of the island and now we're a part of it. She wanted us to be there. I can't believe we are going to be a part of the island from now on. We, of course, aren't Scottish and we aren't descendants of the chiefs, but we know enough about the history here to be a part of it all.

◆ ◆ ◆

We walk back to the Inn Keeper hand in hand. Harry has Rog on the lead. Mum and Dad hug us goodbye in the square and promise to see us tomorrow. We gather together for the service. It's now eleven pm, and the snow is gently falling around us. Children are singing 'O Christmas tree' and it feels festive and special. I can't help but wish that every Christmas will be like this one.

Glenda has told us to come to the Inn Keeper tomorrow with our families before midday, and I'm excited.

A couple of musical islanders are playing instruments on the benches at the edge of the square. Even though it's cold, everyone is feeling festive and jolly.

"I can't believe this is how they do Christmas here," I whisper to Harry, who is swaying next to me. He has a content look on his face while he watches the choir.

"Are you having a good time?" Glenda asks, appearing from nowhere, dressed in a scarf and hat.

"Yes, it's amazing," I say and smile, watching the Christmas tree lights.

"Would you like some mulled wine?" She offers a glass to both of us and stands with us whilst the choir finishes.

"You can join in if you want," she whispers, and gestures for us to go and stand with the school children.

The islanders start playing the instrumental opening to 'Last Christmas' by Wham, and we start singing badly and swaying along while I've got my arms around Harry. I've never loved anyone as much as I love him at this moment, as cheesy as it is. I think it's the atmosphere tonight making me feel like this.

"Thank you, ladies and gentlemen, for that interesting rendition. Now today marks our annual ceremony of the Christmas tree," Glenda starts.

"We welcomed new and old friends to make wishes that we'll now open and if you want, you can share them. As we say every year, nobody has to share their wish- but if you want to and it has already come true from the higher gods or anyone else-" She looks at us and smiles. "We would love to hear it."

"I will start." Glenda opens her envelope and reads it out. "I wish for my son to find happiness and good health."

We all clap, and I see Peter's cheeks redden.

"Whoop, go, Peter," Annie cheers and hugs him and they kiss by the light of the tree.

Hannah steps up to the microphone. "Hi, everyone, my wish wasn't a wish, but I had a gut feeling about a few people here that I wrote down and now I would like to share it," she says, opening her letter.

"I'm getting on now and unfortunately, Simon and I never had any children. We have recently met two bright and friendly souls that I feel I can already trust with my life. My gut was right, and they are amazing people. Harry and Emilia. I would like to welcome you both to the island, and say congratulations to Harry as the new owner of the café." She finishes reading and we all cheer. "Come here, guys." She holds her arms out for us and envelops us in a three-way hug. I still can't believe she has given Harry her café.

"A toast to Emilia and Harry." Glenda comes over and joins in the hug and everyone toasts us. I already feel like I'm a part of the island.

"Harry, Emilia, do you want to share your wishes?" Glenda asks and I nod, not worried at all because mine has come true, and I've seen Harry's and his did too.

"We'll read them together," I say, and we open them at the same time.

"Em." Harry looks up at me.

"Harry," I say back.

"I love you," we both say together, and I see Hannah and Glenda dab at their faces with a tissue. We fall into each other's arms, sharing a kiss in front of the crowds.

Annie, Razor and Tammy come up to us and we all share a hug because they are my best friends and I'm going to miss them even though I know it isn't like we won't ever see each other again.

"I fucking love you guys," I say with tears down my face. It does feel like goodbye. I'm not normally that emotional, well, actually I am, but seeing these notes and, on top of that, being a little drunk, has turned me into a wreck.

"Me too," Annie says.

"Room for another?" Peter asks, and we open our arms to welcome him into our group.

We've had boyfriends and girlfriends come and go, but I feel like Annie might stick with this one.

"To new friends and family," Razor says and we toast again and then Glenda moves us on in case anyone else wants to share anything.

"I have one more thing to say," Harry says. Razor and the others step off the stage.

"Emilia Westbrooks, we've had a wicked time here, and I know nobody says wicked any more," he adds, and I giggle. He carries on.

"I can't describe this adventure we've experienced. It has been a roller-coaster." Harry dips down on one knee and the choir starts again singing 'All I Want For Christmas is You' by Mariah Carey and everyone, including our friends, joins in.

"Emilia Westbrooks, will you marry me?" he says and I immediately say yes with tears streaming down my face. He slips the ring on my finger and it isn't any of Claire's suggestions, thank god. It's a beautiful golden ring with a cluster of diamonds, and I've never loved anything more in my life.

Slowly our friends, and now my mum and dad, Lucy, Dan, and Harry's mum, gather around us and give us hugs. We are all one big happy family.

Even if we live miles away from them, we'll always make the effort to see them. This isn't the end. It's the beginning of another adventure and as I look at Harry, I feel at home and content. I know we've made the right decision, no matter how long it has taken us.

The End

THANK YOU

Thank you so much for taking the time to read my new book. I hope you have enjoyed it. If you would take a few moments, I would really appreciate it if you left me a review.

Amazon

Goodreads

TRADEMARK ACKNOWLEDGEMENT

A Magical Christmas on the Isle of Skye features the following trademarked items… The author acknowledges the trademarked status and trademarks owners of the following wordmarks mentioned in this work of fiction.

Musicians and songs:
- McCartney, Paul. 'Wonderful Christmastime.' McCartney II. *Parlophone Columbia*. 1979. CD
- Slade
- James Blunt
- Wizard
- Kylie
- Los Del Rio. 'Macarena.' A mí me gusta. *RCA*. 1993/1996. CD
- The Cheeky Girls
- Lace, Black. 'Agadoo.' Party Party. *Woodlands studio*.1984. CD
- Steps. 'One For Sorrow.' Step One. *Jive*. 1998. CD
- The Beverley Sisters. 'Little Donkey.' The Essential Beverley Sisters. 1899

- We Three Kings. 1857
- O Little Town of Bethlehem. 1868.
- Beyoncé. 'Single Ladies.' I Am... Sasha Fierce. *Columbia*. 2008. CD.
- 17, East. "Stay Another Day." Steam, London Recordings. 1994. CD
- Wham. "Last Christmas." Music From The Edge Of Heaven, Columbia. 1984. CD
- Mud. "Lonely This Christmas." Lonely This Christmas, RAK. 1974. CD
- Carey, Mariah. 'All I Want For Christmas Is You.' Merry Christmas. *Columbia*.1994. CD
- McArdle, Andrea. 'Tomorrow.' 1977. CD
- Bob the Builder. 'Can we fix it?' Bob The Builder. *BBC Worldwide Music*. 2001. CD
- Bob the Builder. 'Big Fish, Little Fish.' Never Mind the Breeze Blocks. *Universal Music Television*. 2008. CD
- Medley, Bill, Warnes Jennifer. 'I've had the Time of My Life.' Dirty Dancing: Original Soundtrack from the Vestron Motion Picture.*RCA*.1987. CD
- Jones, Tom. 'Leave your hat on.' Full Monty Soundtrack. *Interscope Records* 1997. CD
- Jovi, Bon. 'Please Come Home For Christmas.' Please Come Home For Christmas. *Mercury*. 1994. CD
- Prodigy. 'Firestarter.' The Fat of the Land. *XL, Maverick, Mute*.1996.CD

Companies mentioned:
- McDonald's: McDonald's corporation
- Tesco: Tesco PLC
- BBC 2022
- Feldhues Company
- Buck's Fizz
- Bang On The Door
- Nando's Chickenland Limited
- Hasbro, Inc
- Mattel, Inc
- Kellogg Company
- Christian Dior SE
- Gucci

Films and TV:
- Elf. Dir. Jon Favreau. Perf. Will Ferrell, James Caan, Zooey Deschanel. New Line Cinema. 2003. Picture.
- Rocky. Dir. John G. Avildsen. Perf. Sylvester Stallone, Talia Shire, Burt Young. Chartoff-Winkler Productions. 1976. Picture.
- Bridget Jones's Diary. Dir. Sharon Maguire. Perf. Renée Zellweger, Colin Firth, Hugh Grant. Universal Pictures, 2001. Picture.
- Crane, D & Kauffman, M (Producers). (1994). Friends [Television series]. Burbank California: Warner Bros
- Legally Blonde. Dir. Robert Luketic. Perf.

Reese Witherspoon, Luke Wilson, Selma Blair. MGM Distribution Co. 2001. Picture.
- The Snowman. Dir. Dianne Jackson. Perf. David Bowie (Re-released version). TVC London. 1982. Picture.
- Blair Witch Project. Dir. Daniel Myrick and Eduardo Sánchez. Perf. Heather Donahue, Michael Williams, Joshua Leonard. Artisan Entertainment. 1999. Picture.
- Annie. Dir.   John Huston. Perf. Albert Finney, Carol Burnett, Bernadette Peters, Ann Reinking, Tim Curry. Columbia Pictures. 1982. Picture.
- Moore, C. C., Winter, M., & Merrill Publishing Company,. (1939). 'Twas the night before Christmas. Chicago, Ill: Merrill Publishing Co.

People mentioned:
- Zac Efron
- Elle Woods
- Boris Johnson
- Simon Cowell
- Ross and Monica
- Bridget Jones

ABOUT THE AUTHOR

Jodie lives in a small village in Solihull with her husband and two children. She loves nothing more than dancing around embarrassingly to 90s music and eating mint chocolate. Jodie enjoys reading and writing books full of romance and swoon-worthy fictional men.

SOCIAL MEDIA

To keep up to date with any news on my books or when I will be announcing my next book check out my social media

Twitter; @jodiehomer11
Instagram; Jodie_loves_books
Goodreads; Jodie Homer

BOOKS BY THIS AUTHOR

Raindrops On The Umbrella Cafe

The man of your dreams is one umbrella away.

On inheriting her uncle's beloved Umbrella Café, Sarah packs up and leaves the busy city of Birmingham for her childhood seaside village of Cobble-Heath.

Discovering life at the Umbrella Café is not as idyllic as it was when she was a child. Sarah has to contend with getting to grips with managing a café, accepting her two childhood best friends falling in love and a handsome Australian stranger who has come for the summer. Throw in a family secret with an unexpected arrival and Sarah's life is turned upside down.

Can Sarah keep the cracks in her life sealed up or will she be the next thing to crack up?

Printed in Great Britain
by Amazon